Henry Sewell Stokes

The voyage of Arundel and other Rhymes from Cornwall

Henry Sewell Stokes

The voyage of Arundel and other Rhymes from Cornwall

ISBN/EAN: 9783337017187

Printed in Europe, USA, Canada, Australia, Japan

Cover: Foto ©Andreas Hilbeck / pixelio.de

More available books at **www.hansebooks.com**

RHYMES FROM CORNWALL

By the same Author.

RESTORMEL and other Verses. New Edition, with an engraving of the Castle. Cloth, 3s. 6d.

THE CHANTRY OWL, THE CITY, &c. New Edition. Cloth, 3s. 6d.

THE GATE OF HEAVEN, &c. 1s.

MEMORIES. New Edition. Cloth, 6s.

THE VALE OF LANHERNE, &c. Illustrated by Haghe from drawings by Philp. Royal 8vo. Cloth, 10s. Only a few copies of this edition remain.

BODMIN

PRINTED BY LIDDELL AND SON

THE VOYAGE OF ARUNDEL

AND OTHER

RHYMES FROM CORNWALL

BY

HENRY SEWELL STOKES

A NEW EDITION WITH ADDITIONS

LONDON

LONGMANS, GREEN, & Co.

1884

The present edition comprises The Voyage of Arundel and other Poems published by the late Mr. Camden Hotten in 1871 under the title of 'Rhymes from Cornwall.' To these are now added 'The Knell of Saint Germans' Tower, which was published as 'A Lament for Eliot' with other ballads relating to the Crimean War in 1855; 'The Plaint of Morwenstow,' published separately after the death of the Rev. R. S. Hawker; and the Elegy of 'Lanhydrock,' of which an edition with a biographical note appeared in 1882. A few smaller compositions are interspersed, either not before printed, or taken from booklets of verse now out of print. The frontispiece is from a sketch of the rock called The Armed Knight, near the Land's End, made for this edition by Mr. R. H. Carter of Falmouth, who has so frequently and faithfully depicted the coast scenery of Cornwall.   H. S. S.

Nov. 1884.

CONTENTS.

THE VOYAGE OF ARUNDEL   .   .   I

SAINT GURON   37

SAINTS   41

THE FRIAR'S BONE   46

THE LADY OF PLACE   .   .   53

GALLANTS OF FOWEY   .   .   .   59

COTEHELE   63

BODRIGAN'S LEAP   67

THE WHITE ROSE   .   .   .   71

THE UNGRACIOUS RETURN   .   .   .   74

THE TIMES OF THE CAVALIERS   .   77

ELIOT 93

TRELAWNY 97

VIVIAN . . . . . . IOI

THE SERGEANT 104

THE ROLL CONTINUED . . . 108

THE KNELL OF SAINT GERMANS' TOWER . 110

THE PADSTOW LIFEBOAT 113

THE OLD SWEETHEARTS 118

THE MINER 123

THE BOY AND THE TREE . . . 127

THE PRIDE OF MY HEART IS GONE . . 132

THE DYING MARINER 135

BESSY 136

THERE—NOT THERE . . . 138

WHO NEXT ? 140

IN MEMORIAM W. R. HICKS . . . 143

FATHER AND SON . . . 144

HARVEST, 1864 147

THE SEA AND THE MINER . . . 150

HARVEST MOON, 1876 . . . 151

THE CAPTAIN 160

A SONG FOR SAD MUSIC . . . 165

MARIAN 167

THEY ASK FROM ME A FESTIVE SONG . 169

WELCOME FROM ONE AND ALL . . . 172

THE PLAINT OF MORWENSTOW . 175

LANHYDROCK 181

AN EPITAPH 190

NOTES 191

THE VOYAGE OF ARUNDEL,

ETC.

THE VOYAGE OF ARUNDEL.

I.

A LEGEND of the Western Shore,
Of long-forgotten times of yore,
Shall in my verse an echo find ;
Like distant sound upon the wind,
Or murmur of the ocean wave,
Heard faintly in some inland cave.

II.

Plaintively from Saint Michael's Tower
The chime had knell'd the day's last hour,
And from Saint Mary's chancel grey
The chant was wafted down the bay,

Like anthem from a heavenly choir ;
While, as the crimson radiance stream'd,
The loftier hills as with the fire
Of long-deserted altars gleam'd :
And, white as flakes of ocean foam,
The sea-birds sought their craggy home :
Ships made all sail the port to reach,
And the light shallops climb'd the beach.

III.

Then, as the darkness deepen'd slowly,
Hush'd was each ruder, harsher sound ;
But still those accents sweet and holy
From the high rock with turrets crown'd
Came floating through the stilly air,
Alternate tones of praise and prayer :
Bringing the old man to the door,
Who would ascend the steep no more ;
Reaching the watcher on the cliff,
And the lone fisher in his skiff,
While others near, on strand or sea,
Join'd in the solemn harmony.

IV.

Words such as these 'tis said were sung,
But in another older tongue :—

'Hear, oh ! hear us, Lord of Light !
Ruler of the realm of Night ;
Listen to our suppliant call,
As the darker shadows fall :
On the land and on the wave
From the latent peril save !
Till the night of death is o'er
Keep us, and for evermore !'

V.

So sang they in old England then,
And some ev'n yet respond Amen !
Though few our Pater-nosters now,
An 'Ave !' scarcely ever breathed :
But still instinctively we bow
At empty shrines with ivy wreathed,
Impell'd by mystic sympathy,
Or moved by ' natural piety.'

Arches may fall, and shafts decay,
And all who worship pass away,
The pilgrim 'mid the ruins sighs,
The heart's religion never dies.

VI.

At night, when on the heaving deep
The worn-out winds were lull'd to sleep,
And from St. Michael's lantern far
The light shone like a larger star,
The seaman, as he walk'd the deck,
Thinking the while of storm and wreck,
Would bless the men whose pious care
Maintain'd that friendly beacon there.

VII.

Yet, if old chronicles tell true,
Those times of trustful, steadfast faith
Were days of crime of blackest hue,
Of lawless life and shriftless death.
Then might was merciless as strong,
And unavenged the victim's wrong,

Save by the greater Power unseen,
From whose stern view there is no screen,
No shield 'gainst his omnipotence,
No place beyond his providence.

VIII.

'Twas when young Richard's feeble hand
Scarce grasp'd the sceptre of the land,
From the calm Solent down the sea
A Convoy stood for Brittany.
To aid the Breton Duke was sent
That proud and well-found armament ;
And every ship was taut and staunch,
And fair as builder's craft could launch.
Two hundred men at arms they bore,
And archers twice as many more,
With Knights right worthy of the trust.
Chief in command was Arundel,
Of whom old Froissart's pages tell :
He for his Master took De Rust,
Who of the Northmen's lineage came,
And well sustain'd their Ocean fame.

IX.

Ere night the favouring wind had veer'd,
And towards the Cornish coast they steer'd ;
And, for a while, in the broad bay
That laves the Mount constrain'd to stay,
Angry at their high hopes deferr'd,
Saint Mary's chant they heedless heard :
And, when the beacon shed its light,
Their boisterous mirth disturb'd the night.
At times would fits of laughter peal :
Then from some ship came bursts of song
That almost shook her to her keel ;
So shrill the strain, so deep and strong
The chorus swell'd, as when in June
The kennell'd deer-hounds bay the moon.
Nor till the dawn the orgy ceased ;
Then, as the wind came from North East,
De Rust's white canvas met the gale,
And all the Convoy loosen'd sail.

X.

Grandly and gaily on her course
Moves his tall ship before the blast,
Hail'd by the sea-fowl's welcome hoarse ;
While the red streamers from each mast
Flaunt the bold flock that hover nigh,
'Like snow-cloud in a wintry sky.
And now no more the Mount is seen,
The Madron hills of living green,
And fisher-cots that to the West
Hang on the sea-marge like a nest,
Are past ; and Germoe's shelving coast
Amid the Eastern surge is lost.
Lamorna's cove might tempt her stay,
But fast the ship holds on her way.
And now Saint Levan's granite strand
Rises above the shining sand ;
The Logan, like an uncouth god,
Seems on its pedestal to nod ;
And then Tol Pedn Penwith looms,
Whose cavern many a crew entombs.

B

XI.

The wind veers South, a gale it blows,
And the wild sea yet wilder grows ;
Westward with close-reef'd sail they tack,
And whirling foam-clouds show their track.
Well off Pordenack Point they keep ;
Then with the rolling billows sweep
Where, from the Ocean's depths profound,
Rises the Land's stupendous bound.
Amid the crested waves they see
The Armèd Knight, whose panoply
Of granite will to time's last hour
Be proof against the tempest's power.
Saint Mary's and her Sister Isles,
Where Summer soonest, latest smiles,
They scarcely sight, and Northward steer,
But wide the dangerous Brissons clear.
The ship with the red streamers still
Leads as becomes her Master's skill :
She dips and rises like a bird ;
And in her masts a sound is heard

As in the forests where they grew,
When the strong winds of Autumn blew.

XII.

The Zennor cliffs are hid in spray,
And Morvah seems one sheet of foam,
And when they fetch Porth-Ia's bay
They see the fisher-craft steer home ;
Staunch boats against the stiffest breeze,
And that can live in heaviest seas,
Their crews, as now, expert and brave,
And cradled on the stormy wave.
Warn'd by those wary mariners,
The Master with the Knight confers,
And, rounding the broad Minster sand,
The fleet all tack towards the land,
And where the boats lead on they follow.
Then cheerily the sailors' hollo
Answers the signal to furl sail,
As fiercer blows the adverse gale.
The cables with a rushing sound
Uncoil—the anchors bite the ground ;

And many leave the rolling ships,
As to the sea the red sun dips ;
Some for adventures on the shore,
And some for one carousal more.

XIII.

The Knight, whose ancient name I told,
Was cast in manhood's noblest mould ;
But strong his will, so stern his eye,
That men to meet its glance were shy.
His comrades were of various form ;
All proud of look ; on some the flush
Of youth still show'd so fresh and warm,
That it might match a maiden's blush ;
In others, harder lineaments,
With bearded lip and visage dark,
Told of red fields and sultry tents,
And vice and time had left their mark.

XIV.

Inland their course, they scarce knew where,
And where they went did little care ;

Haply to find some castle hall,

Or hostel snug, ere night should fall.

But soon the skies more darkly lower,

And now bursts down the thunder-shower ;

The wind blows shrill, the lightnings flash,

And the roar drowns the Ocean's din ;

Again the clouds like cymbals clash ;

And ceases—only to begin

Afresh—that combat in the sky.

And whither shall the wanderers hie

For shelter ?—In a leafy wood

There dwelt a holy Sisterhood,

In a lone Abbey, fair to view,

And pilgrims well its access knew ;

Though where its pillar'd arches rose,

No shaft, no stone may now disclose.

XV.

Thither the venturous chief ascends,

Fast follow'd by his troop of friends ;

And through the lowly porch they throng,

When just had clcsed the even-song.

The startled Abbess, pale and saintly,
Looks at each strange, unwelcome guest,
And, as became her, meek and faintly
Asks whence they come, and what their quest.
The Knight replies all courteously,
And pardon for their advent prays ;
They had escaped the angry sea,
And drench'd and cold they need the blaze
Of some kind hearth that fearful night,
And they will leave with day's first light.

XVI.

Doubting what answer should be given,
She would his better thoughts invoke,
And to the Knight aside she spoke :
Reminds him of their vows to Heaven,
Tells him her doubts, and owns her fears,
And with her words she mingles tears ;
And not far distant they would find
A sheltering roof, and welcome kind.
Of no avail her gentle plea
Against his importunity :

The Knight his followers can restrain,
And none will dare that House profane.
Then, with a trembling voice yet clear,
She bids her folk bring wine to cheer—
The wine for way-worn wanderers stored—
And fitting viands for the board.

XVII.

Meanwhile the Sisters, mute and pale,
Have scarcely dared to lift the veil :
The Novices, with beating heart,
Like flutter'd doves, keep far apart.
Others had found safe refuge there
From life's false joy and pleasure's snare ;
Yet long'd of the vain world to hear,
Of friends and scenes to memory dear :
Some of them dames of high degree,
And versed in gentle courtesy.
Of these, some parley with the Knight ;
Some on the bold intruders frown ;
But other eyes, cast meekly down,
Would fill the grave itself with light,

And still retain the dangerous power
They once made felt in hall and bower.

XVIII.

Time flies—how fast the Convent bell
Fails not with punctual voice to tell.
The ladies and the nuns are gone,
To watch, or pray, or dream alone ;
And in the dim refectory
Only the wakeful guests remain.
And well content they seem to be,
To hear the gusts of storm and rain
Rage harmless on the rafter'd roof,
And mullion'd windows, tempest-proof :
Their beakers fill'd with generous wine,
To keep the chill of night away ;
Nor lack they season'd oak and pine,
To feed the blazing hearth till day.

XIX.

The chough sleeps on her shelter'd crag,
The moping owl sits near the ground,

And, later, on the hills the stag
Hears as he thinks the thrilling sound
Of early huntsman's bugle-horn,
The sluggards of the vale to warn.
Certain it is, strange sounds were heard
All through the night from that lone glen ;
And rustics afterwhile averr'd
Their sleep disturb'd by angry men,
By shouts of mirth, or fits of song ;
And then would come a plaintive cry,
As of a night-bird in the sky,
Or wail of woman suffering wrong.
But soon their drowsy senses dull'd,
Till, when light glimmer'd in the East,
And they awoke, the storm had lull'd,
And all those evil sounds had ceased.

XX.

'Tis said by some that at the dawn
The ships and those wild guests were gone ;
But in a script of ancient date,—
And why should time our faith abate ?—

C

'Tis written by a holy man,
Whose page the curious still may scan,
That in the Western harbour lay
The wind-bound ships from day to day,
And that the crews upon them brought
Curses for other outrage wrought.
I may not doubt the old man's word,
Who told and trusted what he heard :
Suffice, that when at last the gale
Seem'd fair, and all the ships made sail,
Others in their dark hulls they bore
Than with them came to that sad shore ;
And all that day, with outstretch'd hands,
Upon the drear deserted sands
The Abbess weeping, watching stood.
So mourns the bird her rifled brood,
No more to gather 'neath her breast,
And hovers near her vacant nest.

XXI.

There is a rock, the seal's safe haunt,
Its sides of heath and lichen scant,

But where its shelly fissures shine
Huge weeds like slimy serpents twine.
Far out it stands in the deep sea,
Yet at low tide it reach'd may be ;
And from its rugged head the view
Extends far o'er the waters blue.
And there that morn a white-robed priest
Was seen, who Westward look'd, and East ;
And then, with hollow voice and stern,
Call'd on the recreants to return :
But short and vague his accents fell,
Soon lost amid the Ocean's swell.
And next he open'd a small book,
And from his breast the Cross he took,
And its gold image in the sun
With a mysterious glory shone.
Then for a time a bell he rang,
But louder peal'd the seamew's clang ;
Nor did his menace more avail
Than the wild whistle of the gale.

XXII.

' O for the Sea ! the wide, wide Sea,
With a gay and fearless company,
In a buoyant ship, with a crowd of sail,
A helmsman sure and a lusty gale !

' 'Tis then, 'tis then the heart leaps up,
The foaming wave is a sparkling cup
To brace the nerves and warm the blood :
All troubles, if any, are drown'd in the flood.

' We laugh, and we quaff, and care not when,
If we ever shall see the land again :
Yet sure if we reach a fresh port to find
The flasks and the joys which we left behind.

' There is a smile on the Ocean's lip,
Though his hug may crush the stoutest ship ;
Who cares—who cares for the coming storm,
So the coast be clear, and the berth be warm ?

' Who sleeps on the shore must have a hard pillow,
For slumber there's naught like the roll of the billow ;

The land has its danger as well as the wave,
And the sea serves as well as the earth for a grave.'

XXIII.

So sang one of those gay compeers ;
They had no qualms, no doubts, no fears ;
Life was to them a summer sea,
Which they meant to sail over merrily.
But otherwise thought the grey-hair'd man,
Who of the ship had anxious charge :
His life had been rough since it began,
Since first he launch'd on the Ocean marge,
A sea of trouble and toil to him ;
And now his day was growing dim ;
The night of death would soon come down,
And he fain would rest in his own old town.
But ask ye how felt those ladies wan,
As the great ships went bounding on,
And who oft look'd back to that dear shore
Which they had left to see no more ?
Say, were they there by fraud or force,
Or wilful took that sinful course ?

Not till the grave shall be unseal'd
Will the dark secret be reveal'd.

XXIV.

Away—away on the open Main,
Like chargers on the battle-plain,
The noble ships went proudly on,
In all their gay caparison.
Like silver manes from their curving bows
The foam flew wild as they plunged and toss'd ;
And then, for a time, as dipt their prows,
They seem'd in the whelming waters lost ;
But soon escaping from the deep,
They gather on the billowy steep ;
Then over the level flood they race,
But De Rust still holds the foremost place.
Arundel's heart is glad once more,
For he will be first on sea or shore.
The Knights all feel like joy and pride,
As they on their Ocean coursers ride :
Some their tall lances grasp, and crave
To tilt upon the rolling wave ;

And one, in his mad chivalry,
Flung his mail'd gauntlet to the sea,
And the sea cast it back to him,
And laugh'd with derision hoarse and grim.

XXV.

Day waned, and wiser thoughts return'd,
And all for some safe haven yearn'd :
Yet on—still on before the wind
They went, but many dropp'd behind ;
And, when it drew towards the night,
Few of the Convoy were in sight.
From his high ship, with serious gaze
Scanning the South horizon's haze,
Look'd forth the veteran Mariner,
De Rust ; and those beside him knew,
Though calm his look, his words but few,
He saw no welcome harbinger.
The petrels dart and dip the wing ;
Upward like shafts the vapours spring ;
A storm will break—it may be near ;
But on the sea he has no fear :

A shallow shore, a rock-bound coast,
The perils which he cares for most.
So spake De Rust ; and he that morn
Did the imperious Knight forewarn
Not to loose sail ; and, when they sail'd,
Again he warn'd, but fate prevail'd.

XXVI.

When the night came, the sea grew calm,
And through the shrouds the trembling stars
Glisten'd as through a Convent's bars ;
But sounds of prayer or holy psalm
Were heard not at the accustom'd hour,
Nor sweet bell chiming in the tower.
Instead a surly bluff command
To heave the lead, or look for land,
Loud oaths, lewd jests, or dreary tales,
And creaking cords and flapping sails.
Then lanterns flamed, and lamps were trimm'd,
And bright eyes flash'd, and goblets brimm'd ;
And lute and viol, glee and song
Made hours like moments wing along ;

Till sin and shame were lapp'd in sleep,
And there was silence on the deep.

XXVII.

When later, in the vault of night,
As in a crypt the taper's light,
The white moon gleam'd, they saw a cloud
Stretching towards them like a shroud ;
And mists at times, like spectres vast,
By them in slow procession pass'd ;
And far away, upon the lee,
Was heard the moaning of the sea.
Well read in signs of wave and sky,
The Master by the helm stood nigh ;
And then a vague presentiment,
The shadow of some grave event,
Came o'er his mind : for his stern creed,
Which with his proof of life agreed,
Taught him, as most too soon will know,
Heaven's wrath is sure, if it be slow ;
Nor is it often long delay'd,
And heavier falls the longer stay'd.

D

And so to him the gathering storm
Assumed the dread Avenger's form.
Yet though he never felt such awe,
Nor may his anxious gaze withdraw
From that strange cloud, he trusts to Heaven
And hopes their sins may be forgiven.

XXVIII.

And soon they hear the booming blast,
But all to meet it is made fast ;
Their upper masts are struck, and steady
Each man is in his place, and ready.
The certain danger makes them brave—
Themselves must aid, if Heaven would save.
No more may they the peril blink—
The storm is on them ere they think !
The cloud is rent, the hailstones crash,
And the fork'd lightnings leap and flash ;
And to the thunders of the sky
The thunders of the deep reply.
May the ship live in such a strife ?
She struggles hard as if for life ;

And, when the waves her decks o'erwhelm,
She springs, and answers to her helm,
As if she knew whose hand was there,
The hand of that tried mariner.
The sailors aid her with a will,
But vain the labour, vain the skill :
Helpless upon the surge she rolls,
With all her freight of sinful souls.

XXIX.

Then, by the trampling over head,
Or by the storm and raging sea,
Or by the ship's great agony,
Or by some innate sense of dread,
The Knight is roused, and all at last
Behold the awful scene aghast.
On the mid-deck a piteous band
Of tremblers, pale and weeping, stand,
Their tresses streaming, drench'd their dress
With seas, while to their hearts they press
The emblem of their dying Lord,
As though 'twould cleanse their guilt abhorr'd.

XXX.

To ease the ship, into the sea
The sailors cast promiscuously
The treasure and the weightier stores ;
But down each hatch the flood still pours,
And in the hold the water gains,
And deeper still she rolls and strains.
Now from the deck hoarse murmurs rise,
Upbraidings shrill, and plaintive cries,
And menaces are mutter'd there.
Then, with white lips that move in prayer,
Though mute, the hapless women kneel,
While skies and Ocean round them reel ;
And then—but how the event befell,
Till the great day may no one tell—
Ere they could breathe a parting word,
Unwarn'd, unshriven, and unheard
Their shrieks amid the billows' roar,
Those suppliants pale were seen no more !

XXXI.

The crimson sun flash'd o'er the flood,
And all the waves seem'd tinged with blood ;

And there the vessel heaved and toss'd,
The masts all gone, the boats all lost ;
And not a ship was nigh to hail,
For all that day they saw no sail ;
And so for days and nights they fared.
Then some few spars the storm had spared
They raised, and other sails they bent,
And the sky did at last relent.
And one bright dawn they saw the land,
When high their drooping spirits rose ;
The Master takes the helm in hand,
And, as the distant peaks disclose,
His grey eye gleams, as when the sight
Of old acquaintance makes life bright.
It was to Erin's coast they bore ;
A bleak inhospitable shore,
Yet blest with harbours safe though few,
Which well the experienced steersman knew.

XXXII.

And now the morning's ruddy streaks
Have reach'd the far Glengariffe peaks ;

And in dim outline from the gloom
Dunkerron's mist-swathed mountains loom.
A forest girdles high Pendeen ;
Below Penmare's deep bay is seen,
And eagles to its hollow shore
Come swooping down from dark Glanmore.
As the light grows more strong and clear,
The Scarriff's jagged rocks appear ;
And far upon the Western verge
The Hermits' lonely Isles emerge ;
Where, guarded by the sleepless waves,
They dwell amid the Ocean caves,
And stranger's step may not intrude
To break their sacred solitude.

XXXIII.

Such was the coast, sublime and lorn,
The shatter'd ship approach'd that morn.
But somewhat now their spirits fell :
So strong the tide, and high the swell,
That it is hard the ship to steer,
Nor may her anchor answer here ;

A sea of shoals and treacherous ground,
And chasms no plummet yet may sound.
And they can see no place to land :
For leagues, all round the rugged strand,
A wall of seething foam extends ;
Above immense the cliff impends,
A mountain-ridge so steep and bare,
The curlew scarce finds shelter there.

XXXIV.

And so the Master told the Knight
'Twere best to hold the open sea,
Yet still to keep the land in sight ;
But the Knight answer'd angrily.
Then to an Islet lying near
He bade De Rust reluctant steer ;
For much he long'd to rest on shore,
His heart was sick, his limbs were sore,
Their wine was spent, their food was scant,
And they had better die than want.
There they might find some kindly folk ;
If foes or pirates there abide,

Better to fall beneath their stroke,
Than perish on the Ocean wide.

XXXV.

With a stern smile the Master hears,
And boldly for the Islet steers :
That there is danger well he knows,
But with the risk his courage grows ;
And hope the passing thought suggests—
Hope ever strong in manly breasts—
They there may find some shelter'd bay,
Where the storm-stricken ship may stay
If but few hours ; and they meantime
Would trace the path the Islesmen climb.

XXXVI.

Fast the ship nears the place, and now
The breakers rise above her bow ;
But the high rocks on either side
Scarce leave a passage for the tide.
One chance—the last ! on sand or rock
To beach her—will she bear the shock ?

Onwards she cleaves, the white sands gleam,

And shrill the startled sea-mews scream ;

But on the deck no voice is heard

Except the Master's warning word.

Unblenching in the face of Death,

He, while the seamen hold their breath,

Bids them all now for death prepare :

For there the Avenger stands—ay, there !

Not in the sky as on that night,

But in broad day, in all men's sight ;

He now waits for them on that shore—

'Tis there—'tis there Heav'n's thunders roar !

XXXVII.

As the keel grinds along the beach,

A path between the rocks and sands

They see, and think they all may reach ;

And first on shore the Master stands,

To test the dangers of the place :

Others rush by as in a race,

And straggling climb the craggy steep,

And midway drop into the deep.

E

The rest still cling about the wreck ;
But now the billows sweep the deck,
The waters rush through all the seams,
And rend the ribs, and lift the beams.
And then, upon the breakers thrown,
Some grappling sink, and some alone ;
Others ashore like shingle whirl'd,
Then back into the breakers hurl'd.
Some, who were lost amid the surge,
Far out from watery depths emerge ;
Some, where the dark abysses yawn,
Down—down by slimy creatures drawn.

XXXVIII.

One stalwart form a rock did clasp
With arms so stout, the billow's grasp
Awhile seem'd foil'd, so strong was he,
But vain his strength aganist the sea.
On the sharp rock where he had clung
His body, breathing still, was flung ;
Then to and fro 'twas dragg'd and dash'd,
Till every bone and muscle crash'd.

So perish'd grand and good Musard,
Whom *sans reproche* did all regard.
That he deserved a happier doom,
And other grave than Ocean's tomb,
Many might think, but Heaven knew best,
All pray his soul in peace may rest !

XXXIX.

But where the Knight—the Master where ?
De Rust, known by his silver hair,
Guided the few who faintly strove
To mount the path from that wild cove.
And Arundel had climb'd the sand,
But high above him rose the strand ;
Yet there, as if secure, he stood,
And calmly view'd the angry flood.
The Master saw, humane as brave,
And turn'd once more to face the wave ;
From crag to crag he fast descends ;
Soon from the beetling ledge he bends :
The lifted hand he seizes now—
Thick sweat-drops falling from his brow—

Safe ! safe !—the caves their cheers resound :
When, by a sweeping wave's rebound
Caught up, while still their hands held fast,
They both into the gulf were cast.

XL.

A few faint shouts, some stifled moans,
And all was hush'd, save the fierce tones
Of waves that held the quivering prey,
Or shriek of birds that bore away
Their portion of the ghastly feast.
Save these all other sounds had ceased :
And of the ship no spar was seen
To tell that she had ever been.

SAINT GURON.

I.

Turn back, turn back the page of Time,
And read or sing some older rhyme,
Of days when yet the daisied sward
Had not become this green Church-yard,
Long ere these hillocks broke the ground,
Where thousands now in death sleep sound.
Thousands ?   Ay, thousands : who may tell
How fast and thick the people fell ?

II.

Thousands ? yes, thousands I repeat :
Here, as one day this path my feet
Paced with the Vicar of the Church,—
A man of rare and quaint research,

Of Cornwall who, and Cornishmen,
Knew more than any living then,—
He ask'd how many here might lie,
And waited long for my reply.

III.

The area scarce two furlongs fetch'd,
But wide I knew the Parish stretch'd ;
I counted generations past,
And made my reckoning up at last,
And told : our figures well agreed,
That in this little grassy mead
Twice twenty thousand dead are hid,
Enough to build a pyramid.

IV.

Long, long before one turf was turn'd,
While still some Pagan altars burn'd,
Perhaps while yet on Caradon
The Druids' mystic rites went on,
A stranger came and built his cell
Near where those bubbling waters well,
Which then were but a crystal rill
That flow'd between each wooded hill.

V.

A fitter spot in that wild age
Was nowhere found for hermitage ;
And there he tarried many a day,
Alone to fast, alone to pray ;
And when from villages far off
Rude stragglers came to stare and scoff,
He met them with meek courtesy,
And words of humble piety.

VI.

He told them how to a far land
One came, who with a loving hand
Did heal the sick, and help the poor ;
Who bade the sinful sin no more ;
Did in his arms the children bless,
And spoke to all with tenderness ;
Weeping with those who mourn'd their dead,
Until his own dear blood was shed.

VII.

So did the lowly Hermit preach,
And much they marvell'd at his speech :
But when he taught them how to pray,
And use the words our Lord did say—

' Our Father !'—then they wonder'd more,
They never heard the like before ;
And soon their hearts began to move,
And feel for God a filial love.

VIII.

One day they came, and found him gone !
Elsewhere to pray and fast alone,
Or speak to others like sweet words.
They only heard the summer birds,
And streamlet murmuring through the dell,
And then they felt they loved him well ;
And by his name they call'd the spot,
Nor will it ever be forgot.

IX.

Few were the listeners then, where now
Near his lost cell a thousand bow,
To hear the name of his dear Lord ;
And round the Church* in the green sward
Twice twenty thousand Christians rest ;
And, his blest mission to attest,
A building stands with open door
For the sad Orphans of the Poor.

* St. Petrock's Church, Bodmin.

SAINTS.

I.

If Scotland be the Land of Cakes,
The Land of Saints must Cornwall be ;
More than a summer's day it takes
To spell their hard orthography :
The list exhausts the Alphabet ;
Their names in sequence due to set,
And tell their acts as should be told,
Would task Saint Alban's Monks of old.

II.

But names uncouth and quaint had they,
Or strangely maul'd by rustic jaws :
Saint Teath, Saint Breock, and Saint Day,
Saint Veep, Saint Feock, and Saint Mawes ;

F

Saint Wenn, Saint Kew, and Simonward,
Alias Saint Breward ; and, as hard,
Saint Enodock, more soft Saint Issey,
Saint Ewe, Saint Ive, and Mevagissey.*

III.

But stay, the names would fill a book,
I mean the names 'tis said they bore ;
And some, perchance, for Saints men took,
Who little of Saints' semblance wore.
Dark was the age, the people rude,
They trusted more than understood ;
And had meek Wesley then appear'd,
He had been as a Saint revered.

IV.

Each parish had one Saint at least,
But when they came, or of what race,
From North or South, or West or East ;
Whether from Germany or Thrace ;
Greek, Roman, Saxon, Celt or Dane ;
Whether from Africa or Spain,
Or Ireland, where 'tis said they swarm'd,
We never shall be well-inform'd.

* See note, Saints.

V.

Linguists and archæologists
Are now indeed so clever grown,
No tangle but their skill untwists ;
For hours they will discuss a stone,
As did the famed Pickwickians once ;
Who can't read Aryan is a dunce ;
Some from a brick an empire rear,
And others make the Sphynx speak clear.

VI.

Truly our ' savans ' have learnt much,
Yet may have something more to learn ;
Their sketches yet may need a touch,
Or the dim lines to blanks may turn.
Quick—quick to save the trace ! the gloom
Grows thick as shades in Pharoah's tomb :
Few are the foot-prints on Life's shore,
And Time's dark tide sweeps all before.

VII.

Others as idols worship now
The fading memories of the past ;
To mental images they bow,
That once in ruder moulds were cast.

With awe they gaze at crumbling stones,
They kiss the dust of dead men's bones ;
They hate the new and loathe the strange,
And think the world should have no change.

VIII.

Many are just the other way,
They little care for former things,
No homage to the past they pay,
But catch each bubble as it springs.
A busy and a dizzy age,
Few now will con the musty page ;
The railway cleaves through hallow'd ground,
The Earth in steam-clouds whizzes round.

IX.

Some would a middle course pursue,
And naught that's human hate or scorn ;
They love the old, may like the new,
Though much in old or new they mourn.
If somewhat slow to bend the knee,
They venerate authority ;
And when the ancient paths they tread,
They render honour to the dead.

X.

Respect to those call'd Saints we pay,

Though none would that high prefix claim ;

The missionaries of their day,

We bless and thank them in God's name.

Call or miscall them what you will,

They did their Master's word fulfil ;

And He will own their work well done,

Though Saint and sinless was not one.

THE FRIAR'S BONE.

I.

EIGHTH of the name, bluff Harry reign'd,
  A King most grim and bold,
And how he kill'd his lovely wives
  Still makes the blood run cold :
I may not dwell on those dread scenes
  And crimes of days long gone,
But hasten by, and for my text
  Take up a dead man's bone.

II.

His must have been no common form,
  His height six feet might be ;
And by the size I may surmise
  ' A manly man ' was he :

Haply in sandals stalk'd the deer
　　With Bodmin's booted Prior,
And yet as well as surpliced clerk
　　Could preach this rope-girt friar.

III.

No more of him, his name is lost,
　-　And by his side in heaps
His fellows lie and moulder on,
　　And none their record keeps :
Like them their faith forgotten here,
　　Though, in these latter days,
Some say the ' dry bones ' move, and soon
　　Will the fall'n altars raise.

IV.

Mine is a vision of old times,
　　And here, where now I stand,
The ancient Convent rears once more
　　Its outline fair and grand ;
And through the pictured windows streams
　　The soften'd summer light ;
Nor shut they out the heavenly rays
　　That pierce the cloud of night.

V.

Again I hear the matin chime,
    Again the vesper bell ;
And at the noon of night once more
    The solemn anthems swell :
I see the long procession form,
    With emblems lifted high,
When view'd by all with reverence
    The solemn pomp goes by.

VI.

In the dim cloisters one might find
    Old scripts of learning rare,
Well-conn'd by some who wore the cowl,
    And then found only there :
And where from out its ivy shroud
    Yon crumbling chantry looks,
A tonsured sage to studious youth
    Taught from those priceless books.

VII.

Yonder—well named of Lazarus—
    Where now no stone remains,
Others, skill'd leeches, would repair
    To ease the sick man's pains ;

And at the Convent's vaulted door,
　　Early and late thrown wide,
The hungry waited, nor in vain
　　The weak for succour cried.

VIII.

Beneath their high and ample roof
　　The weary pilgrim slept,
When he had shared the liberal fare
　　And generous wine there kept :
The scholar poor and wealthier guest
　　Needed no hostel then,
Sure of a courteous welcome kind
　　From those secluded men.

IX.

The vision fades, and other scenes
　　Rise from the shadowy past ;
I hear bold Luther's gospel trump,
　　And Hal's defiant blast :
Then suddenly succumbs the King,
　　The Pope's most doughty Knight,
Struck by a flash from Anna's eyes,
　　That beam'd with heavenly light.

G

X.

'Tis an old tale, that woman's charms
    Have baffled Courts and Schools ;
Her smile has set the world on fire,
    And made the wisest fools :
But Henry was no Solomon,
    And nothing like so amorous :
And then he had a sterner way
    Of silencing the clamorous.

XI.

Priests, monks and friars, a motley swarm,
    Attack'd him with fierce railings ;
Though not a few, like Abelard,
    Had human nature's failings :
But why repeat Polwhele's queer tales,
    Or turn to Rabelais' stories ?
In every age and clime men cry
    ' O tempora ! O mores ! '

XII.

Enough of that. Like thunderbolt
    At last the fiat came,
Pope Henry's Bull, and ruthlessly
    They did enforce the same.

Short time had monks and friars to quit
  Their consecrated walls,
Their cellars and refectories,
  Their libraries and halls.

XIII.

Hast been in Tintern's roofless aisles,
  On the fair banks of Wye,
Or stood 'neath Glastonbury's arch,
  With no regretful sigh ?
If so, though else we well agree,
  We'll travel different ways ;
For to my view o'er all the past
  There rests a tearful haze.

XIV.

Who shared with owls the vacant piles,
  Who got the broad demesnes,
Though it would not take long to say,
  My flagging rhyme refrains.
Here, vagrants occupied the cells,
  Tipplers were set in stocks,
Pigs 'mid the graves were penn'd, and kine
  Low'd to the bleating flocks.

XV.

In after years the Convent roof
    Echoed the trumpet's sound,
When with the Sheriff's bristling troop
    The red-robed Judge came round.
But now of church, halls, cells and graves
    There scarce remains a stone !
Stones have preach'd sermons, and here ends
    My sermon of the bone.

THE LADY OF PLACE.

I.

FIVE hundred years and more ago,
 Third Edward ruled us then,
From Fowey near fifty ships set sail,
 With nigh eight hundred men :
No other Port on England's coast
 An equal force could bring ;
For Calais when they weigh'd, they form'd
 The Vanguard of the King.

II.

And when of Henries reign'd the Sixth,
 The ships of Fowey went forth
To every sea, and every shore,
 East, West, and South, and North .

And the Bay was like a forest
　For tall and stately masts,
And flags of many countries
　Came with the veering blasts.

III.

The Fowey men grew so haughty,
　They would no bonnet veil ;
But the folk of Rye and Winchelsea
　Would make them dip the sail.
And on a day, to settle it,
　They fought both man and boy ;
And from that time those Cornish lads
　Were called Gallants of Fowey.

IV.

Still more they fell to merchandise,
　And prouder still did grow :
Their cruisers harass'd all the coast
　From Cherbourg to Bordeaux.
But one dark night, when scatter'd far
　Their ships on Ocean wide,
A sound as from a cloud of sails
　Came with the flowing tide.

V.

The Lady of Treffry remain'd
    In her large mansion lone ;
Her husband to the distant chase
    With horse and hounds had gone.
The watch-dogs bark'd ; then shouts—then shrieks
    Rose from the sleeping town ;
The vengeful French, like unloosed fiends,
    Went ranging up and down.

VI.

Here torches flash'd, there sledges crash'd,
    Such was their devilish game ;
And soon from many a house-top
    Burst out the crimson flame.
As in broad day men saw the bay,
    The ships, the shores, the towers ;
Then blinding clouds of smoke came down,
    And red flakes fell in showers.

VII.

But she was there, that Lady,
    To play no woman's part ;
Though the great sufferings of her town
    Had pierced her gentle heart :

And Fowey men, like a wall of steel,
   Though few, about her stood ;
While some, to cut the ships adrift,
   Crept out upon the flood.

VIII.

And on the wharves, and in the streets,
   Was heard the awful clang
Of swords and weapons strange ; with fist-
   Some on the Frenchmen sprang ;
Some met them with a Cornish grip
   They never more forgot ;
And many found the Cornish hug
   Much rougher than they thought.

IX.

But other were the scenes and sounds
   Of that unhappy night,
When, like a flock of bleating lambs,
   By the burning roof-trees' light,
Mothers their wailing children led
   Through wood and shelter'd lane,
And up the winding moorland paths
   Which to this day remain.

X.

Still calm look'd forth the Lady
　　From her embattled wall ;
Her presence was a power, her voice
　　Thrill'd like a trumpet's call.
˙Meanwhile the bells kept tolling,
　˙To rouse the country round ;
And spires and turrets far away
　　Sent on the warning sound.

XI.

And long before the daylight
　˳Fires lit the lofty peaks ;
˳And men were moving in the vales,
　　And stirring in the creeks.
Small need—so brave that Lady proved,
　　The Fowey gallants so true,
That at cock-crow, like baffled wolves,
　　The Frenchmen all withdrew.

XII.

Whether a panic seized them,
　　I will not pause to learn ;
They had done enough of mischief,
　　And might perhaps return.
H

But, when they went to find their ships,
   The Fowey folk laugh'd outright ;
For some were scuttled, some aground,
   Some drifting out of sight.

XIII.

Next morning with his Posse
   The Sheriff came at dawn ;
The flames still roar'd, the French on board
   The ships they saved had gone :
Three cheers, then, for the Fowey gallants !
   For the Lady three times three !
And, if the French should come again,
   May our wives as fearless be !

XIV.

Changed is the world, much changed since then,
   Yet will they come once more ?
Who knows—or cares—or fears ? who doubts
   We'll serve them as before ?
Grace Darling died but yesterday,
   And others of her race
May yet be found to emulate
   That Lady brave of Place.

GALLANTS OF FOWEY.

I.

GALLANTS of Fowey ! gallants of Fowey !
Good hands to get freights or take prizes—Ahoy !
Though I hang for it shortly, I'll hazard the trip,
And be one of the crew of that sea-going ship.

II.

The anchor is up and the harbour-chain down,
And the bells they ring merrily out from the town ;
We shall soon find a Spaniard or Frenchman, they
    say,
And bring something back to this snug little bay.

III.

To take from such prowlers it can be no crime,
We've no letters of marque, but can get them next
    time :

So away ! and at last we are out on the sea,
And the cliffs of Old Cornwall fade fast on the lee.

IV.

And bold is our Captain as ever set sail,
As brave in a fight as he is in a gale ;
He sunk a big galiot when last he went out,
And the cheeses and Dutchmen went bobbing about.

V.

A sail, boys, to windward, which soon we'll o'erhaul,
Set royals and spanker, and studding sails all ;
She sees us, and seems in no haste to escape,
A fine Spanish gallion in rig and in shape.

VI.

But our Captain looks ugly the nearer we come,
He whistles and swears—then gets awfully glum ;
We are caught ! 'tis a frigate ! her colours display'd
Show she comes from the land where those cheeses
        were made.

VII.

A shot from her stern-port comes bowling along,
She'll take us and keep us, I'll bet you a song :

Our Skipper at once sends his flag to the peak,

And all of a sudden grows civil and meek.

VIII.

Their boats have now reach'd us, the pick of the
crew,

All arm'd to the teeth, with lieutenants no few ;—

'What's your name ?' Quoth Mynheer, as he
muster'd his men,

'Honour'd sir,' said our Skipper, 'I'm Captain
Polpen.'

IX.

'And where do you hail from, and where are you
bound ?'

'From Fowey, sir, I come, and must make Plymouth Sound,

And thence to the Scheldt for a cargo of cheese,

And here are my papers, to see, if you please.'

X.

'I see,' said the Hollander, with a queer smile,

'But I think you'll be safer with us for a while ;

Your pikes, guns, and swivels, and shot so well
    ranged
No doubt were to be for Dutch cheeses exchanged !'

XI.

And then to the Scheldt without stopping we went,
But not with our will, and to prison were sent :
'Twill be many a month ere I shout ' Ship Ahoy !'
A long, long good-bye to the sweethearts of Fowey !

COTEHELE.

I.

It was a wild and lawless time,
And what was virtue might be crime,
Açcording as opinion veer'd,
Or as the helm of State was steer'd :
But men were earnest, fierce and strong,
Whether the cause was right or wrong ;
They had small tenderness for foes,
And their best arguments were blows.

II.

Where between leafy uplands glides
The Tamar with her changing tides,
Kissing the shores of either shire,
Until she meets her Ocean sire,

There, high above the girdling wood,
Cotehele's quaint mansion long has stood ;
Just as it is, four centuries past
It look'd, and will as many last.

III.

Firm is its grey embattled wall,
The rusted armour crowds the hall,
And the queer carven furniture
Doth still the worm's slow tooth endure :
The storied tapestry still hangs,
Scarce injured by the moth's keen fangs ;
And on the stout-limb'd board remain
The cups our fathers loved to drain.

IV.

When to Cotehele the tidings came
That Richmond's fleet had pass'd the Rame,
Edgcumbe* with red rose wreathed his crest,
And join'd the rising in the West ;
But driven from Severn's flooded shore,
He cross'd again the trackless Moor,
And in his woods on Tamar's strand
Waited and watch'd—with sword in hand.

*Richard Edgcumbe, of Cotehele, Knighted on Bosworth Field.

V.

And now it was the quiet hour
When twilight steals through hall and bower ;
The curfew from the turret peal'd,
The gate was closed, the flask unseal'd,
And strains of antique minstrelsy,
And tales of love and chivalry
Made the bright moments glide too fast,
When—hark !   A clarion's warning blast.

VI.

Who comes so late and knocks so loud,
And why with him that armèd crowd ?
Slow is the warder to unbar,
Till he can make out who they are :
But soon he sees stern Bodrigan
Is there with all his ruthless clan ;
Nor waited Edgcumbe more to know
Why came so late his deadliest foe.

VII.

Brave as he is, he may not stay
And keep those ravenous wolves at bay ;
But through the woods he flies to reach
The Rock above the Tamar beach,

I

Where now the little Chapel stands ;
Built later by his grateful hands,
And which for ages yet will be
Memorial of his piety.

VIII.

'Tis gain'd—his foes are at his heels,
Their panting breath he almost feels ;
He springs—no more they see his form,
Though on the giddy ledge they swarm ;
But in the twilight dim and grey
They see his headgear float away,
And laugh and say the man is drown'd,
To-morrow will his corpse be found.

IX.

Ha ! ha ! But Edgcumbe he laughs too,
For far across the waters blue
Next morn his boat was scudding free
To the safe shore of Brittany.
Ha ! ha ! he lives and may return,
And in his breast, as in an urn
Of smouldering fire, his wrath will keep
Him mindful of that frightful leap.

BODRIGAN'S LEAP.

TEMP. HEN. VII.

I.

FROM Bosworth's gory field where lay

    His King a mangled corse,

With many a dint Sir Harry* came

    Upon his barbèd horse ;

Which all that day in that fierce fight

    Had proudly carried him,

But Westward now must bear him fast

    Across yon mountains dim.

* Sir Henry Trenowth of Bodrigan, also called Sir Harry Bodrigan.

II.

Through the dark hours he still rode on,
  With followers few and faint ;
Resting brief while in forest drear
  By well of some old saint :
On—on from day to day they fared,
  Shunning each bower and hall,
Until they sight one starry night
  Bodrigan's Castle wall.

III.

The Knight's clear blast is answer'd fast,
  And blithe the warder greets him ;
And with a smile and with a kiss
  His Lady-love soon meets him :
And in that high embrasured tower
  His war-worn limbs may rest ;
For place like that for wealth and power
  Was not in all the West.

IV.

And many a century it stood
  To prove its ancient fame,
Though but some lowly walls now bear
  Bodrigan's honour'd name.

Its princely hall, its bastions strong,
  Its chapel turrets fair
Are gone like cloud-built palaces,
  And castles in the air.

V.

Not long the respite : on his track
  The Tudor's warhounds follow,
And soon in Cornwall's rocky glens
  Reverberates the view-hollo.
Foremost two mail-clad horsemen spur,
  Trevanion of Carhayes,
And Edgcumbe of Cotehele, who now
  Bodrigan's raid repays.

VI.

The Knight looks forth, and in his park
  He sees their gleaming crests ;
And knows them, and their purpose stern,
  Nor waits for his old guests :
But by a secret way, alone,
  He leaves his hall for aye,
And for the headland makes that hangs
  Over the Gorran bay.

VII.

But soon they find the path—he hears
  Their rapid footsteps nigh,
And from the headland leaps, while shrill
  The baffled hunters cry.
In the dark sea they think him drown'd,
  As on the giddy steep
They stand and look, and only see
  The waters wild and deep.

VIII.

They look'd and jeer'd, and made the shore
  Ring with their angry shout ;
And still they look'd, perchance to see
  His dead bones toss'd about :
And then they saw a boat dash through
  The surge, and as she went
The rescued Knight above the roar
  His parting curses sent.

THE WHITE ROSE.

I.

From Scotland came the Lady bright
Who did her troth to Warbeck plight,
Thinking him true Plantagenet,
As many will believe him yet :
A dame she was of high degree,
And fair, ay, passing fair to see ;
And, for her beauty and her fame,
' The White Rose ' came to be her name,

II.

Well did fair Cath'rine love her lord ;
And when he girded on his sword,
And donn'd his helm, so like a prince
He look'd, the sight would all convince.

So when she saw the nodding plume,
The royal mien, the manly bloom,
Proud as the lovely Trojan dame
Was she whom all 'the White Rose' name.

III.

His purpose as his peril great,
He must away to find his fate ;
While she upon the 'guarded mount'
Must many a weary moment count.
Forth as he went to test the land,
His Lady waved her lily hand,
Looking, as there she stood, the same
' White Rose' as when she gain'd that name.

IV.

He went—but never to return !
Proud was the Tudor's heart and stern ;
Their task the Judges may not shirk,
The axe must do its hideous work.
The Lady by the Cornish shore
Shall wave her lily hand no more,
But weeps and weeps, yet none dare blame
That still ' the White Rose' is her name.

V.

Even the King the name approved,

And his hard heart in pity moved,

To see on that fair cheek the blight

Changing the red rose into white :

And since that hour the scent still grows,

In memory's urn, of that pure rose ;

And to this spot* none ever came

But call'd 'the White Rose' by her name.

* St. Michael's Mount.

THE UNGRACIOUS RETURN.

TEMP. ED. VI.

I.

I HAVE a startling tale to tell
Of what in Bodmin town befell
In the distant time long, long ago,
When every man was his neighbour's foe,
And lords like tigers prowl'd the land,
Each with his own well-chosen band,
To do his work of savagery ;
When Princes fought for sovereignty ;
Who loyal was to day, to morrow
Might be call'd traitor to his sorrow.

II.

Three centuries since, at Bodmin town,
When sturdy Boyer wore the gown,

The Royal Provost wrote a line
He on a day with him would dine,
And begg'd he would meanwhile prepare
A gibbet for some rebels there.
The Mayor obey'd him to the letter,
Thinking the stronger side the better ;
And, with his maces, at the gate
His Worship did his guest await.

III.

And then into the Common Hall
Mayor, Provost, Aldermen, Burghers all
Went with a rush and made good cheer,
On beef and venison, wine and beer ;
And many a loyal toast was given,
And fear and doubt away were driven
With bumpers full and foaming high :
Yet wicked look'd the Provost's eye,
But he laugh'd, and did not spare the sherry,
Which made his host feel proud as merry.

IV.

While thus they revell'd within, without
Hammers were heard, until a shout

Told that the gibbet was up ; and then
Forth came the Mayor and Aldermen,
And Burghers all, with the Provost stern,
Who had set his mind to make return
To the Mayor for his hospitality ;
And how 'twas done you soon will see,
For on the gibbet, at his own door,
His Worship swung in a moment more !

SIR BEVILLE.

Sir Beville Grenville was a Knight
  By all true men beloved,
And, noble as his lineage was,
  His nature nobler proved.
To lead the chace, a court to grace,
  Or deck a lady's bower,
Beyond compare ; of chivalry
  All own'd he was the flower.

Country and King to him were dear,
  And he had served them both,
And in the council and the field
  Had shown his love and troth.

Eliot and Hampden were his friends,
   But best he loved the King,
And in the days of his distress
   To him must only cling.

One morn a dark cloud cross'd his brow,
   As he, with paces slow,
Left his broad park, and bade adieu
   To his fair place at Stowe.
' Knight of the Sorrowful Countenance '
   He might be call'd—so sad
His aspect was, and so distraught,
   Some thought him almost mad.

'Twas thinking of his hapless King
   That made Sir Beville grieve ;
And nothing but the clash of swords
   His anguish could relieve.
And he shall have enough of it,
   Ere many days are past—
It sounds ! his champing war-steed hears
   The distant trumpet's blast.

ANTHONY PAYNE.

But who of Anak's mighty mould
　　Came with the sombre Knight ?
No fabulous form, but flesh and bone,
　. Seven feet scarce reach'd his height :
His chest as ample as his girth,
　　And that nigh two yards round ;
And, when he spoke or laugh'd, his voice
　　Did like a mastiff's sound.

His hug was like a bear's, and him
　Not Polkinghorn might throw ;
And with his fist he could knock down
　　A bullock at a blow.
His sword was made to match his size,
　　As Roundheads did remember ;
And when it swung 'twas like the whirl
　　Of windmills in September.

And for a bouse and long carouse
　　He was at all times ready,
But never yet was tankard found
　　To make his gait unsteady.

His head was large, with crisp brown curls,
  And had no lack of brain ;
A comely and a witty man
  Was stalwart Anthony Payne.

Such was his stature and his form :
  As for the horse he rode,
You may be sure it was not small,
  And bone and mettle show'd ;
Deep chest, short pastern, and high crest,
  The mane was silver white,
And the broad flank of dappled gray
  Shone like his armour bright.

And to the wars he in his youth
  Would with Sir Beville go,
Whom well he loved, for he was born
  Near by the House at Stowe :
Sir Beville's son grew up with him,
  And they were just as brothers ;
In sports a-field and manly games
  They each excell'd all others.

THE RENDEZ-VOUS.

At length near Launceston's grand old Keep
　　Sir Beville's troop drew rein,
As did the gallant Company
　. That follow'd in their train :
And there with loyal Hopton,
　　And his good men and true,
They all shook hands, and raised a shout
　　That pierced Dunheved through.

Then came still night ; but from the Keep
　At times would roll a psalm,
　And then a song from Grenville's camp
　　Would break the awful calm ;
But over all Payne's master voice—
　　A voice to shake the steeple—
Shouted the name of Charles the King,
　　And cursed all crop-ear'd people

When morning tinged the Eastern hills
　　Some toward the Tamar rode,
Which like a stream of silver sheen
　　Through the dark valleys flow'd ;

L

And when they reach'd the Cornish bank,
   As Lifton chimes rang seven,
Sudden they saw the gleam of pikes
   In the green woods of Devon.

Horsemen and pikemen cross'd the ford,
   And midway came together,
Like two fierce herds in narrow space
   That meet in sultry weather :
They long'd to break each other's heads,
   But Payne, such calves' play scorning,
Laugh'd loud, and wheel'd, and some shook hands,
   And each bade each 'good morning !'

Of bootless strife from day to day
   I little care to tell ;
Some, after combat, met as friends,
   And wish'd each other well :
They toasted, drinking from one cup
   The nut-brown beaded ale—
' Let's settle it by a toss,' quoth Payne,
   ' How say ye, head or tail ?'

A huge grim Roundhead answer'd ' Head ! '
 And head it proved too soon ;
And then they laugh'd, and then they quaff'd,
 Till rose the crescent moon :
But rough their kindness was—a word
 Might turn it into wrath ;
There was stern purpose in their looks,
 And danger in their path.

STAMFORD HILL.

The year was sixteen—forty-four,
 The day sixteenth of May ;
'Tis well to keep such dates in mind,
 If not the hour, the day.
On Stratton Hill (since Stamford call'd)
 Earl Stamford's forces throng,
To battle for the Parliament,
 Well nigh five thousand strong.

The King's force number'd less than half,
 On scanty rations kept ;
All fared alike, the chiefs and men,
 And none that night had slept.

Among the leaders Cornwall gave,
　　Godolphin and Mohún,
Grenville, Trevanion, Basset, each
　　Had loyal service done.

So led, four several ways they climb
　　The memorable hill :
Again, and yet again they rush,
　　Hurl'd back and rallying still :
For foes as sturdy held the height
　　As those who tried to take it ;
The tramp of thousands round the hill
　　Did like an earthquake shake it.

And now, about three hours past noon,
　　The assailants cease their fire,
And with their faces to the foe
　　With firm slow step retire.
Their ammunition spent, they halt,
　　But, when the word is given,
Their swords ' outface ' the musketry
　　Which darkens all the heaven.

Before that rush Earl Stamford's troops
   Fall back in sullen rage,
Save Chudleigh's pikemen tall and grim,
   Who closer fight will wage ;
And when the daring Cornishmen
   Have reach'd the hill's steep marge,
Upon them with a mighty shout
   The furious pikemen charge.

Then down went foot and horse, and down
   With them Sir Beville went ;
But to his aid the giant strode,
   And such good succour lent
With his long arm and sweeping sword,
   The Knight sprang up, and then
Cheering and cheer'd on his strong horse
   Spurr'd to the front again.

Not slow the Cornish follow him,
   Their track a crimson stream,
Till on the hill at once the helms
   Of the four columns gleam :

And there they meet, and there they greet,
  And then their mingling ranks
Grasp hands, and all together cheer,
  And all to God give thanks.

LANDSDOWN.

The months speed on, and runs my rhyme,
  But troubles rend the land ;
And many an Englishman must yet
  Fall by a brother's hand.
They gather now in every shire,
  And all the people arm ;
And now is heard from hill to hill
  War's shrill and strange alarm.

They were not ranged by party cries,
  Or stirr'd by hustings-slang ;
The brawl of factions had been hush'd
  By the first trumpet's clang :
And friends were foes, yet still were friends,
  And all in God did trust ;
The mingling life-blood seal'd each cause—
  Blest be their mingling dust !

It was the same unhappy year,
  July the Fifth the day,
To Lansdown Hill each army march'd,
  All in complete array,
Well-mann'd, well-horsed, well-fed and fresh,
  And eager for the work ;
In either host not one that day
  His dreadful task would shirk.

At break of dawn the enemy
  Gave proof of Waller's skill ;
When, as the morning breeze sprang up,
  The mist swept from the hill.
Upon the brow high breastworks rose,
  And cannons' muzzles show'd :
Which seen, the royal force faced round,
  To find a safer road.

That instant Waller's cuirassiers
  Were launch'd on rear and flank ;
The Royal squadrons fronted them,
  But down went rank on rank :

Calm Slanning with his rolling fire
  Does now the shock receive,
While Maurice and Carnarvon's swords
  Their old renown retrieve.

The Cornish musketeers push on,
  And wing the rallying horse ;
And baffled the grim cuirassiers
  Retrace their blood-mark'd course.
Loth to look on, the Cornish foot
  Claim next the right to move—
' It is our turn,' cried One and All,
  ' Our loyalty to prove.'

And leave is given, and up the hill
  They spring like hounds in cry,
And from the flanking woods stern forms
  Greet them as they go by.
Horsemen and footmen upward press,
  As it had been a plain,
Till down the iron-mail'd troopers come,
  And cleave their front in twain.

Then Grenville spoke, whose sword as yet
    Had not one morion cleft :
His horsemen now he placed to right,
    His musketeers to left ;
Midway he led his pikes,—his son,
    A youth, did with him ride,
And Payne, whose spear look'd like an elm
    Torn from the mountain-side.

Right up before the cannon's mouth
    And breastwork's storm of shot,
With firm sure steps they mount the hill,
    Their sweat-drops falling hot.
Twice had the Ironsides charged their ranks,
    And still they moved unbroken ;
Upwards, though falling fast, they urge,
    And not a word is spoken.

Once more—the third—oft final time,
    Those awful Ironsides crash ;
Rings Cornwall's cheer, and Grenville's sword
    Gleams like a lightning flash :

M

On—on he charged, and still he spurr'd,
    And still his sword was gleaming,
When horse and rider fell, and fast
    His own life-blood was streaming.

But Payne was nigh with that brave youth,
    To hear his parting words ;
Each stoop'd and kiss'd his clay-cold lips,
    And then they clench'd their swords ;
And fiercer yet the battle raged,
    As Cornwall's shout went up,
And from the hill-top ran the blood
    Like red wine from a cup.

The work is done, the height is won,
    But vengeance goads them still—
' Halt men, let God avenge ! ' so said
    The Knight on Stamford Hill :
As if he spoke they now obey,
    And scarce believe him dead,
Till with moist eyes they turn and pass
    By Grenville's gory bed.

L'ENVOY.

Ah ! gentle Lady, far away
In Stowe's fair mansion lone,
Widow'd like thee will Cornwall grieve,
. And England hear thy moan.
Payne with the sorrowing youth brings back
The dead to his own place ;
But yet a harder task it is
To brook that weeping face.

And from that time the love between
Sir Beville's son and Payne
Grew stronger, stronger every day,
Till death should snap the chain.
In many a hard-fought field they charged
As brothers, side by side ;
And grieving sore from Marston Moor
They did together ride.

And when the King was doom'd to die,
The last dread act to view,
Before Whitehall there tower'd a form
Whose features some there knew.

When fell the axe, a curse was heard
  Loud as a lion's roar ;
A moment, and a dark shade pass'd—
  The form was seen no more.

Years roll'd, and reign'd the Second Charles,
  And in the Palace-yard
The loyal, fearless Cornishman
  Stood tallest of the Guard ;
Nor fail'd he then to like good ale,
  Or brighter sherris quaff,
And fling around his merry jokes,
  And make the gay King laugh.

Peace to his grand heroic soul !
  Peace to his ashes vast,
Which now in Stratton Churchyard rest,
  Waiting the trumpet blast
To call him to a loftier field,
  Where war shall never rage,
And all the brave and true and good
  Will dwell for endless age !

ELIOT.

' THE most illustrious confessor in the cause of liberty whom that time produced.'—*Sir John Eliot, a Biography, by John Forster.*

I.

O WORLDLING of this giddy hour,

O toiler of this busy day,

And ye who hold the helm of Power,

And ye who seek to have the sway,

Say, have ye thought, had Heav'n assign'd

Your fate to live in that stern age,

How would ye each have been inclined ?

Would Royal smiles your hearts engage,

Or Freedom's ruder impulse move,

And would your deeds your bias prove ?

II.

Men acted their convictions then,
And on their conscience staked their all,
Land, life, and liberty, like men,
Resolved like men to stand or fall.
So Hampden, Falkland, Grenville did,
And Eliot, neither last nor least,
Whose name will shine till truth is hid,
And right and freedom both have ceased ;
Till the wave leaves the Island shore,
And England England be no more.

III.

Go, read the page that tells his life,
Go, read his words that plead for him,
For you, for all who in the strife
'Twixt Might and Right, till suns grow dim,
Must mix and mingle day by day.
The strife at times may be less hard,
The glory less : but 'tis no play
This life of ours, as some regard,
But hath its purpose grave and just,
And duties high and solemn trust.

IV.

The language Eliot spoke we breathe,
The manliest language of the World,
And which our sires to us bequeath
To spread with England's flag unfurl'd
The speech of freemen to all lands :
A tongue of something more than sound,
Moulded not more by lips than hands ;
Than other speech less sweet and round,
But fraught with eloquence of deeds,
A living page to him who reads.

V.

Words may be deeds—such Eliot's were,
'Stablishing liberty and law :
They made men's hearts within them stir,
And thrill'd the misled King with awe,
And turn'd his ill-advisers pale ;
Yet that they came from loyal breast
As Grenville's own, whom none assail,
Let Grenville's love for him attest.
Oh ! had the King but listen'd then,
There had been joy for all good men.

VI.

While song and story proudly tell
Who glory won with lance or sword,
Others as bravely stood or fell.
The field, where Hampden's life-blood pour'd,
Think ye, was that more hallow'd ground
Than the low dungeon, dark and chill,
Where Eliot pined as years roll'd round ?
The axe could not more surely kill :
They kept him there to die—and there
They dug the martyr's sepulchre !

VII.

Such was the fiat harsh and blind !
Ay, gaol the dead, if so 'tis doom'd,
But there is that no chain may bind,
The thought that cannot be entomb'd ;
The deathless words, the eternal truth ;
The actions of the wise and just,
That wear an everlasting youth ;
The worth that cannot turn to dust.
So, Eliot ! lives thy patriot name,
Nor needs a Milton for its fame.

TRELAWNY.

Sir Jonathan Trelawny, Bart. Consecrated Bishop of Bristol,
November 8, 1685. Committed to the Tower with the
Archbishop and five other Bishops, June 8, 1688. Tried
and acquitted, June 17, 1688. Afterwards Bishop of Exe-
ter, and translated by Queen Anne to Winchester. Died
June 31, 1721.

I.

'Tis a good name, as well hath sung
    The bard of Morwinstow ;
It will not die, the reason why
    All Cornish people know :
Nay more, 'tis written on the page
    Of England's high renown ;
Undimm'd Trelawny's name will shine
    Till Britain's star goes down.

N

II.

A faithful Bishop and true Man,
  Of Cornwall's oldest stock,
Against despotic James he stood
  Firm as the Land's last rock.
As brave, but in a holier cause,
  As in far times of yore,
When lance and shield at Agincourt
  Sir John Trelawny bore.

III.

One of the memorable Seven,
  Who went at that dark hour,
While soldiers knelt and thousands wept,
  Into that fatal Tower.
And then I see them with the throng
  Come to the Minster Hall,
While far away the angry cry
  Swells up from One and All !

IV.

The people wait the verdict long,
  But now at last 'tis given,—
' Not Guilty ! '—with a mighty shout
  The lofty roof is riven.

And onward rolls that burst of joy
   Through all the teeming streets ;
East, North, and South it spreads, and West,
   Till Cornwall's cheer it meets.

V.

And never now that glorious Hall
   With lingering feet I tread,
But in my ear the shout resounds
   That hail'd each mitred head.
Oft as I pace the Cornish heath,
   When no one else is nigh,
The voices of the past repeat
   ' Trelawny shall not die ! '

VI.

But he has left us more than fame,
   His own blood still beats here ;
His race inherit his good name,
   And love what he held dear.
Not only here, throughout the land
   England's great heart beats on ;
And ' Earth's blest blood ' still circulates,
   As in the ages gone.

VII.

Go where you will, in every shire
  Immortal memories dwell,
That of the men of days gone by,
  And some still living, tell.
The influence breathes in all the air,
  You'll meet it on the wave,
In Minster aisle and Village Church,
  And at the common grave.

VIII.

The Spirit of our Sires has cross'd
  The broad Altantic Main ;
It finds its way down Southern Seas,
  And thence it comes again.
From Westminster to Washington,
  From Cornwall to the Tower,
'Tis just the same, with change of name,
  Up to this very hour.

VIVIAN.

Lieut.-Gen. the Right Hon. Richard Hussey, Baron Vivian of Glynn and Truro, G.C.B., &c. Born at Truro, July 28, 1775. Died August 20, 1842.

I.

Worthies of Cornwall ! long the Roll
That bears your proud historic names,
Blazon'd with many a famous scroll,
And making good wild Cornwall's claims
To rank with England's fairest shire,
For all that noble souls admire.

II.

The Roll dates from the distant age
Of Arthur and his Chivalry,
Who on the Laureate's epic page
Rise from the dark oblivious sea,
While looms again the vanish'd Tower,
With all the glories of that hour.

III.

Grand as those shadows of the past,
Vivian ! to me thy form appears,
Though but a shadow now, and fast
Fading into the gloom of years :
Yet some that form in memory bear,
Which might with Rome's high race compare.

IV.

No arm more puissant than thine
Bore lance, or did a falchion wield,
With the Red Cross in Palestine,
At Poictiers or on Crecy's field :
Naseby and Flodden could not show
More gallant knight, more generous foe.

V.

What fields the Cornish soldier fought,
What laurels won, what medals wore,
What names were in his banner wrought,
Were long to tell : the stars he bore,
Shining like rays from Glory's wings,
Were gifts of Nations and of Kings.

VI.

Marlborough would have honour'd him,
As Wellesley did with no faint praise :
One greater still, whose star grew dim,
Saw through the battle's lurid haze
How. Vivian, as the trumpet blew,
Led the last charge at Waterloo.

VII.

From pealing domes and festal halls
He hasten'd to his native town,
While thousands gather'd round its walls ;
And less he prized the world's renown
.Than Cornwall's greeting, when once more
He reach'd Saint Mary's rippled shore.

VIII.

Years pass—sad change comes o'er the scene ;
Through a mute crowd the sable plumes
Move slow where he so cheer'd had been :
No drum is heard, no cannon booms,
As home, among his kin to rest,
They bring the Warrior of the West.

THE SERGEANT.

'Twas autumn—clouds on clouds were piled,
And the sear leaves went whirling round ;
When a lone horseman from the wild
Sought shelter from the storm, and found
In a low shed a grey-hair'd man,
Who plied his saw and plane with skill,
Though maim'd and halt, but turn'd to scan
The wanderer's looks, who watch'd him still.

II.

The horseman said, ' Your wood is rare,
And from no English forest came :'
The man look'd up with a proud air,
And call'd it by its Spanish name.

' And where learnt you that foreign speech ?'
' I learnt it under Sir John Moore,
When Soult just gave us time to reach
And get away from Spain's hot shore.

III.

' And soon we saw the English coast,
And in the Downs for weeks we lay,
But might not land ; we long'd almost
To take French leave, and steal away.
Word came, and back with merry hearts
'Cross Biscay Bay to fight we went :
I mind it when my old wound smarts,
In where the Frenchman's steel was sent.

IV.

' 'Twas at Vittoria I was hit
By one of Joseph's grenadiers ;
I left my marks, but now was bit,
And there I lay, while with loud cheers
My Regiment charged, and since that time
I have been lame.   Of God I crave
Pardon, for sure it was a crime
To slay such handsome men and brave.'

o

V.

' Have you a pension, friend? ' was ask'd.
' Yes, it was small ; but on a day,
Years back when I was sorely task'd
To get my living, rode this way
The hunters, each in scarlet coat,
And with them General Vivian came,
Who stopp'd, sir, at this very spot,
And call'd for me by my own name.

VI.

' I had served with him, and I told
How hard the times were, and he said
He'd not forget his comrade old,
And smiling left me—he is dead !
But he spoke for me and was heard :
My pension soon was raised, and I
Knew it was due to his kind word,
And I shall love him till I die.'

VII.

'Twas half in sorrow, half in mirth,
The old man spoke, then talk'd of Spain
As fairest country on the earth,
Then in the chestnut drove his plane ;

And then went back to some great fight,
And seem'd his Captain's voice to hear,
And stretch'd his limb and stood upright,
And look'd a British Grenadier.

THE ROLL CONTINUED.

I.

Time wears not out the pedigree :
  Boscawen dies, and Pellew vies
With him for glory on the Sea,
  Algiers' dark cells his noble prize :
And Reynolds, none than he more brave,
Who sleeps beneath the Baltic wave.

II.

Yon lofty landmark of the West,
  The stranger asks the cause and name?
The graven lines with truth attest
  How Gilbert earn'd his martial fame
In Eastern battles fierce and long,
Aye foremost in the combat's throng.

III.

Not yet extinct the dauntless breed,
  As shown again and yet again,
Whenever England stands in need ;
  With the ' Six Hundred ' charged Tremayne ;
At Inkerman an Eliot fell,
As bleeding hearts too truly tell.

IV.

I name but few to prove the race ;
  Mine is no Battle-Abbey Roll,
And none would care to find a place
  In my poor perishable scroll :
And this is sure, that England's fame
Will never lack a Cornish name.

V.

The war-clouds gather round us now,
  But England's sword rests in its sheath ;
Yet, let a warning trumpet blow,
  Let but a sound of menace breathe,
And Cornwall's sons not last will be
To charge with England's chivalry.

THE KNELL OF ST. GERMANS' TOWER.

———

Captain the Hon. Granville Charles Cornwallis Eliot, of
the Coldstream Guards, second son of the third Earl of
St. Germans, fell at Inkerman Nov. 5, 1854, in the 26th
year of his age.

I.

The leaves know not their time to fall,
And so death happens to us all :
But leaves are shed when they are sere,
In the dark season of the year ;
Our blossoms fade as well in spring
As when away the swallows wing ;
Ev'n while our hopes are fresh and green
They drop, and sadden all life's scene.

II.

Light was his step, the tears were few
When high-born Eliot bade adieu !
Though not because the love was less,
But in the bloom of manliness,
And in the glow of martial pride,
It were unseemly to have sigh'd :
Like one who heard a marriage-bell
He went, and breathed a gay farewell.

III.

Ere long there came from o'er the sea
Tidings of glorious victory :
Again, and yet again, the bells
Pour'd their blithe music down the dells,
And from the Land's End to Cotehele
Seem'd in glad rivalry to peal ;
But silent was St. Germans' tower,
For gloom was there in hall and bower.

IV.

And then it peal'd a slow sad knell,
And people said, he nobly fell
With the brave Guards, who form'd the van
At the great fight of Inkerman !

The death was grand, the cause was just ;
Agreed—but that bright form is dust !
And lofty phrases serve but ill
The void which death has made, to fill.

V.

Yet was it truly, kindly told,
That now, as in the times of old,
Our Nobles heed the Country's call ;
In Castle grey and sylvan Hall,
At War's alarm their proud hearts bound,
And soon their life-blood dyes the ground :
Such is our English Chivalry,
This—this is true Nobility !

THE PADSTOW LIFEBOAT.

February 6th, 1867.

I.

I sing no more of belted knights,
  Or the pure blood they boast ;
My song is of the sterner stuff
  That guards our native coast :
The hearts of oak that grow all round
  The Islands where we dwell,
Whose names have less of Norman sound,
  And easier are to spell.

II.

At Nine A.M., wind West North West,
  And blowing half a gale,
Round Stepper Point a Schooner came,
  But under close-reef'd sail.

P

'Tis a wild place to fetch, the waves
  Break on the Doombar sands,
And from the hills the eddying winds
  Perplex the steadiest hands.

III.

And now she glides in water smooth,
  But the ebb-tide runs fast,
And suddenly the land-wind blows,
  And shakes each bending mast :
Soon back to sea she drifts away,
  Nearing Saint Minver's shore ;
Then grounds, and o'er her deck the high
  Atlantic billows pour.

IV.

Man, man the Lifeboat ! Many a crew
  Her pride has been to save
In a stronger gale and darker hour,
  And from a wilder wave.
Their names are : Harris, Truscott, French,
  Hills, Cronnell, Brenton, May,
Varcoe, Bate, Bennett, Malyn, and
  Intross and coastguard Shea.

V.

All trusty men of pluck and strength,
  And skill to guide withal ;
Some more than some had proved their worth,
  As chance to them did fall :
Shea for his humane chivalry
  The Imperial medal wore ;
Intross and Varcoe's breasts the words
  ' Crimea,' ' Baltic,' bore.

VI.

One more, Hills claims brief mention here,
  No sturdier man than he ;
In quest of Franklin's bones he went
  To the dread Arctic Sea.
Such was the staple of the crew,
  Who work'd with earnest will ;
To see them breast the awful waves
  Made the spectators thrill.

VII.

Toward the ship their way they cleave,
  But may not reach her side ;
And then to Polzeath bay they steer
  Against the wind and tide :

And now the breakers as they burst
    The buoyant boat submerge ;
O'erturn'd she rights, and then again
    Heels in the whelming surge.

VIII.

The watchers from Trebethick Cliff
    And high Pentire rush down,
As dead or gasping on the rocks
    The dauntless crew are thrown.
Of the thirteen but eight survive !
    Shea, Truscott, breathe no more ;
Varcoe and Cronnell, last Intross,
    Come lifeless to the shore.

IX.

The Schooner's crew, five souls in all,
    Save one the shore did reach,
Just where the stranded vessel lay
    On the Trebethick beach.
He, at the moment when she struck,
    Was jerk'd into the wave ;
And well he swam in sight of all,
    But none was nigh to save.

X.

The wail of widows pierced the night,
    And on the star-lit strand
The weeping children, fatherless,
    Still linger'd, hand in hand.
And love and pity thrill'd men's hearts,
    For sorrow makes all kin ;
And not to honour bravery
    Were more than shame—were sin.

XI.

Soon to the old Church-yard the dead
    'Went with a countless throng ;
All but the splendid Irishman,
    So gentle, brave and strong :
And him to lone Lanherne they took,
    Where manly tears did fall,
While other rites his ashes bless'd
    Within that ancient wall.

THE OLD SWEETHEARTS.

I.

I HAVE a curious tale to tell,
   Beyond all contradiction ;
Perhaps you'll laugh, you scarce will weep,
   But truth's more strange than fiction.

II.

Long years ago, a maiden fair
   Dwelt in a Cornish village ;
An honest man for spouse she chose,
   Who earn'd his bread by tillage.

III.

'Twas said she liked another more,
   But that was country scandal ;
Though some one else had courted her,
   Who well the plough could handle.

IV.

He was the younger of her swains,
   Stout wrestler and good dancer ;
But why the elder gain'd the day,
   ·Is more than I can answer.

V.

For that, or for some other cause
   'Tis needless to unravel,
The youth resolved to cross the sea,
   And try the effect of travel.

VI.

He had warm friends, and they shook hands,
   And, when at last they parted,
His rival's wife gave him a kiss,
   And he went off down-hearted.

VII.

But she was faithful to her spouse,
   And bore him children plenty ;
And all grew up, and married, most
   Before their years were twenty.

VIII.

The man and wife lived cheerily
  Some fifty years together ;
And then he died, but she seem'd like
  Some winters more to weather.

IX.

But what became of her first love
  Across the stormy ocean ?
He was a widower old and rich,
  In the new land of Goshen.

X.

And from him to his ancient flame
  There came one day a letter ;
Which to the dear old lassie proved
  He never could forget her.

XI.

Her years fourscore—so comely still,
  Her age no one could guess it ;
She wrote an answer with firm hand,
  And neatly did address it.

XII.

Ere she expected, o'er the sea
  He came, no youth was defter ;
Thinking, no doubt, throughout the voyage,
  To find her as he left her.

XIII.

And so, perhaps, the widow thought
  To find her former lover ;
But when they met and kiss'd, alas !
  A change did each discover.

XIV.

Said he—' Who cares for lapse of years,
  For change of form or feature ?'
' The heart's the thing, my own true love !'
  Replied that kind old creature.

XV.

Their time was short to coo and court,
  So for the ring he hurried ;
Married they were, but few were there,
  Just all their friends were buried.

Q

XVI.

And then, to spend the honeymoon,
They cross'd the broad Atlantic :
As yet they have no progeny,
So ends my tale romantic.

THE MINER.

I.

His form is spare, his look sedate,
   His cheek is pale, his eye is bright ;
He rises early, rises late,
   Turns night to day, and day to night ;
And half his life lives underground,
And so his weary years roll round.

II.

'Tis his to find the glittering ore,
   For ages hid in earth's dark womb ;
To creep and climb, to dig and bore,
   And build himself a living tomb,
Some six feet high, some four feet wide,
And reach'd o'er depths that few would stride.

III.

He toils as most are doom'd to toil,
    Not for his own but others' wealth ;
Just as the ploughman turns the soil,
    But this man's bread is bought with health :
So few his years, his heart would sink,
Cared he of such sad themes to think.

IV.

If England's Church is for the Poor,
    The Miner scarcely knows the way ;
His Chapel seen on every moor
    From Hingston Down to far Cairn Brea ;
Built by his own and comrades' hands
The plain and lowly temple stands.

V.

What's more, he both can pray and preach,
    It was Saint Wesley taught him how :
His voice is strong, and plain his speech,
    His style not graceful I allow ;
Much like the manner it may be
Of the poor folk at Galilee.

VI.

He takes his text from the same book
    As the great lawn-sleeved Doctors read ;
A shepherd, but without the crook,
    His sheep are sometimes wild indeed,
The outcasts often of the poor,
Too shabby for a Gothic door.

VII.

When his work's ended, and he dies
    Much short of three-score years and ten,
Hundreds with honest tears and sighs
    Will gather—maidens, mothers, men ;
And, as his toil-worn limbs they bring,
They sing the hymns he loved to sing.

VIII.

But I've not done with him as yet :
    He or his seed is in all lands ;
His hand the Chilian ores must get ;
    On Chimborazo's range he stands ;
Australian, Californian gold
Tells where a Cornishman takes hold.

IX.

His arm is strong, though spare his form,

His eye is clear, though pale his cheek,

If cold his hand, his heart is warm—

To find his like you far must seek :

Should he get rich in other Zones,

To Cornwall he brings back his bones.

THE BOY AND THE TREE.

I.

'Twas in a shelter'd Cornish vale,
Where the young elms grow straight and strong ;
Where earliest blossoms scent the gale,
And birds delay their parting song :
From the dark wood with infant glee
Leaps out and laughs the dimpled river,
Regardless of the angry sea,
In which its mirth will cease for ever.

II.

And not far off a grey Church-tower
Its form like some tall patriarch rears ;
Whose voice has told the passing hour
Some say for twice three hundred years.

For ages folk have gather'd round
Those walls when chimed the sabbath warning,
And in these cots has buzz'd the sound
Of cheerful toil at early morning.

III.

Inland one day in leafy June
A sea-cloud like a billow roll'd,
And, as from an eclipse at noon,
Its shadow fell on grange and fold.
Then burst the storm, the lightning flash'd,
The thunder drown'd the ocean's roar,
Against the tower the hailstones crash'd,
And then the Sun shone out once more.

IV.

But prostrate on the greensward lay
One tree amid its forest peers,
Just now as high and fair as they,
And like to bide the blast for years.
Oh ! it was sorrowful to see
Those branches sear'd, those roots uptorn ;
And all that lofty company
As for a brother seem'd to mourn.

V.

The dews wept for its fall at eve,
Birds sought in vain its boughs at night,
And never more its vernal leaf
Would whisper welcome to the light :
But truce to fancy, and your pity
For other themes and woes reserve ;
That stem may help to build a city,
Those limbs into a ship may curve.

VI.

Bring, sturdy swains, your axes bring,
Nor let the log the earth encumber :
A sapling in its place shall spring—
Nay, what is one in such a number ?
Trees in their fate resemble men,
Nature to each short respite granting ;
Down to the dust they drop, and then
Not long will any find them wanting.

VII.

Another morrow dawn'd, and fast
His gleaming steel each hewer plied ;
The schoolboys, as they frolick'd past,
View'd their prone friend, and paused and sigh'd.

R

Some loiter'd even while the bell
Sternly its ninefold knell deliver'd ;
The final stroke that moment fell,
The roots recoil'd, the huge trunk quiver'd.

VIII.

One from his place that day was miss'd,
A merry, bright-hair'd, blue-eyed boy ;
Whose cheek that morn his mother kiss'd,
Whose step at noon would bring her joy :
She listen'd—but no step she heard
When the bell chimed the mid-day hour ;
She watch'd and listen'd till the bird
Return'd at twilight to its bower.

IX.

Then on each mind sad bodings came,
And old and young, in ardour vying,
Went forth, and search'd, and call'd his name,
But no one heard his voice replying.
Some ranged the hills and moorlands far,
While others paced the dingles hollow ;
And one pale form by Eve's wan star
Did to the shore the streamlet follow.

X.

In vain they sought him many a day ;
On groaning wains the tree was lifted,
And, where it once so grandly lay,
In heaps the Autumn leaves were drifted.
A guess into conviction grew,
And to the spot the people hurried,
Where digging deep,—most strange but true,—
Under the roots they found him buried !

XI.

Why was it, when the thunder broke,
That tree was from the rest selected ?
Why fell the hewer's final stroke
When the fair boy no harm suspected ?
That mother's form, it haunts me still,
And still I hear that wail of sorrow ;
The purpose must be left—until
On Earth shall dawn the eternal morrow.

'THE PRIDE OF MY HEART IS GONE.'

I.

A LITTLE cot with a garden plot,
  And a wall-flower by the door,
Under a hill where sea-birds shrill
  For ever dive and soar ;
A form once fair, now worn with care,
  By the hearth sat chill and lone ;
A heavy tread, and a voice that said—
  ' The pride of my heart is gone !

II.

' I have lost my lad and all I had,
  And he was my only son,
And the woman there no other will bear—'
  She sigh'd ' God's will be done ! '

' God's will,' cried he, half angrily,
    ' To God himself is known ;
I only know the wind did blow,
    And the pride of my heart is gone !

III.

' But yesterday in Saint Ives' broad bay
    Was moor'd my staunch sea-boat ;
No fairer craft, both fore and aft,
    On the brine did ever float :
I stood on the beach as she left the reach
    With all her canvas on ;
But never more will she make the shore,
    The pride of my heart is gone !'

IV.

Just as he spoke a large tear broke
    Away from his stern dark eye ;
And I turn'd aside, not to wound his pride,
    And heard the woman sigh :
But soon the man again began
    To tell, with a stifled groan,
How the skies did frown, and the storm came down,
    And the pride of his heart was gone.

V.

'Twas a fearful night, no star, no light,
　　As they the Channel cross'd ;
And the gale each hour gain'd greater power,
　　And the waves more wildly toss'd :
What next befel he could not tell—
　　Sigh'd she, ‘ God's will be done ! ’
He bow'd his grey head, and only said—
　　‘ The pride of my heart is gone ! ’

THE DYING MARINER.

Bless the Lord, O my soul : and all that is within me, bless
his holy name.—Ps. 103, v. 1.

THOSE words he utter'd, when by anguish bow'd,
Yet with firm hand he sign'd his brief last will :
Few were his earthly chattels, fewer still
The savings to his honest thrift allow'd,
Tho' he for threescore years the deep had plough'd,
Had proved all climes, and weather'd many a gale
Beneath bare poles or under close-reef'd sail,
And when his hammock might have been his shroud.
But God, he said, was with him all his days,
Nor would forsake him now on the dark shore ;
And then, with a clear accent, he once more
Repeated David's grateful song of praise,
And like a prophet's voice across the Sea
Sounded that dying mariner's homily.

BESSY.

I.

A TENDER, bright-eyed, dimpled child,
She sat upon her mother's knee :
On all who smiled on her she smiled,
Or to their arms went trustfully,
No prettier fledgling in the nest,
No sweeter bud on woman's breast
      Than darling Bessy.

II.

She grew, and bloom'd into a flower,
Which other bosoms long'd to wear ;
A fragile rose from Eden's bower,
That needed gentlest, fondest care :

And one came by, who saw and sigh'd,
And woo'd and won her for his bride,
  The blushing Bessy.

III.

And with the swallows soon they went,
To find a sunnier, milder clime,
And there they stay'd with sweet content,
As did the swallows for a time,
And built their nest ; and one bright morn,
'Mid pains and tears and smiles was born
  A second Bessy.

IV.

A shadow cross'd the summer land ;
By a lone tomb a soldier weeps,
No more to kiss the gentle hand
So lately link'd to his !—She sleeps,
But hard and cold and lone her bed :
Oh ! bitter, bitter tears were shed
  For dear lost Bessy !

THERE—NOT THERE !

I.

'Tis night—the travellers by the train
Disperse, and seek their homes again
Through streets now vacant, dark and cold,
Where life's flood-tide that day had roll'd.
One walks apart, and needs no ray
To guide him on his lonely way,
No graven lines to tell him where
The old house stands—'tis there ! ay, there !

II.

He reaches soon the outer wall,
He now hears footsteps in the hall,
And at the sound his bosom yearns ;
But, when at last the slow hinge turns,

No look of welcome meets his eye,
Strange voices to his words reply ;
He fain would climb the oaken stair,
But those he looks for are not there.

III.

There many a year his kin had dwelt,
His mother in yon chamber knelt,
Lisping by her own mother's knee
The prayer she taught his infancy.
Both have long slumber'd in their graves,
One near, one far across the waves,
But he will no denial bear,
And looks for those who are not there.

IV.

The bells in the Cathedral Tower
Toll as of yore the passing hour,
And through the night those weary feet
Move not beyond that crypt-like street.
The steam-blast shrills, the spell is o'er,
The traveller speeds from that closed door,
But often through the murky air
Looks back, and sighs for those not there.

WHO NEXT?

I

THE man was pale, his steed was fleet—
He stopp'd amid the busy street—
A few brief hurried words, and fast
Onward the boding horseman pass'd,
As one who shunn'd some foe's pursuit,
Leaving his startled listeners mute ;
Till each, as with the shock perplex'd,
Inquired of each—' Who next, who next ? '

II.

Some silent to their homes retired,
And there, as of themselves, inquired
' Who next ? '   And others on their way
Along the peopled street did say

' Who next ? ' and scarce could tell the tale
Which made that hasty courier pale ;
But still, as with the shock perplex'd,
They question'd each they met—' Who next ?'

III.

How blithe and clear on that same morn
Was heard the huntsman's bugle-horn !
The horse stood ready for the chase,
But vacant was the rider's place :
Sudden the dismal post went by,
And ceased at once the field's full cry ;
And each, with grief and awe perplex'd,
Demands of each—' Who next, who next ? '

IV.

Oh ! strange that he should thus have died
At fortune's noon, in manhood's pride ;
From his domain so large and fair,
From all that claim'd his thoughtful care,
And all that nearest clasp'd his heart,
Forced by that fatal stroke to part !
By Heaven's severe decree perplex'd,
We hardly dare to think—' Who next ? '

V.

Who next ?   Ay, let the words go round,
Though harsh and ominous the sound ;
Who next ? the infant and the sire,
The old man and the youth inquire ;
Who next ? let whispering lovers ask ;
Who next ? the reveller through his mask :
The solemn preacher, as his text,
Asks of the shuddering flock—' Who next ? '

Feb. 24, 1854.

IN MEMORIAM W. R. HICKS.

'Alas,poor Yorick !—I knew him, Horatio.'
HAMLET.
'I declare I know not, Yorick, how to part with thee.'
STERNE.

Adieu ! dear, genial, faithful friend, Adieu !
Courteous as witty, nor less wise than gay ;
The debt for happy hours we owe to you,
Time will not cancel, nor may tears repay.
Your presence brighten'd many a gloomy day :
At humbler doors, or 'neath the pillar'd hall,
How glad the host who heard your footstep fall,
How pleased could he the parting word delay !
We miss you—miss you at the social board ;
We miss your taste in the saloons of Art ;
We miss your touch, when Music strikes the chord ;
When troubles come, we miss your head and heart :
And last, most precious tribute at life's end,
The poor still grieve for you as their lost friend.

Sept. 5, 1868.

FATHER AND SON.

I.

Once more, my trembling hand once more
Would wake the chords that long have slept :
But, if the strains were sad before,
The saddest for the last were kept :
In vain I strive to change the theme
I learnt in early years too well,
As floating down life's troubled stream
I ever hear the plaintive bell.

II.

Again it sounds, where yon high tower*
Stands like a prophet old and grey,
And, though no clouds of winter lour,
Deep gloom pervades the land to-day.

* Lanlivery Tower.

Oh, piteous sight ! between the hills
Two hearses winding dark and slow,
While every heart that meets them thrills,
And every eye is dimm'd with woe !

III.

The son came home, how changed and worn
With the wild tumult of the Sea !
And in his father's arms was borne
Up to his chamber tenderly :
Beside him watch'd a loving band,
And, as the patient sufferer smiled,
The mother smoothed with gentle hand
The pillow of her dying child.

IV.

Not yet—not yet, though soon to part,
A greater trouble must precede,
A deeper anguish rend each heart,
So hath mysterious Heaven decreed.
The Father dies—the dying son
Becomes the widow's comforter,
And cheers the others one by one,
But may not his farewell defer.

T

V.

'Tis over—and they bring them now,
The white-robed priests their coming meet ;
Bare-headed all the people bow,
To hear the words so grand, so sweet,
That speak of death as blessedness ;
Sighs and responses swell around,
Till to the tomb the mourners press,
And dew with tears the hallow'd ground.

Feb. 2, 1869.

HARVEST.

1864.

' And, behold, Boaz came from Bethlehem, and said unto
the reapers, The Lord be with you ; and they answered,
The Lord bless thee.'—RUTH.

So spake, as in the Sacred Page is told,
The master and the men in times of old,
With courtesy and kindness, in God's name,
When the glad season of the harvest came ;
And what prevents like greetings should again
Be heard between the master and the men,
When in fair England, at the day's first beam,
The reapers' scythes among the cornfields gleam :
Calling on Him who still the pledge fulfils,
And spreads his harvests on a thousand hills ?

God speeds the plough—the furrow opens wide
As, with a practised eye and measured stride,
The peasant drives his patient team a-field,
Till the low sun sinks like a crimson shield.
The sower next his lighter labour plies,
When winds blow chill, and clouds invest the skies ;
The broken clods the scatter'd grain defend,
Till wintry snows their softer shelter lend,
While the log kindles, as the blithe Old Year
Dies, and fond memories gather round his bier.

But soon again, at the appointed hour,
The streams dissolve, and falls the genial shower ;
The song of birds is heard, and from the soil
The lengthening stalk makes glad the heart of Toil.
By fervid suns the Earth's chill breast is warm'd,
The blossom bursts, the pensile ear is form'd ;
And on a day, at Heaven's serene command,
The golden ranks stretch o'er the peaceful land :
Then the lithe reapers like an army rise,
And in long lines the ripen'd harvest lies ;
And soon the sheaves, along the hills and plains,
Are borne like trophies on the groaning wains.

Manners with times may change, but while the ground
Renders her fruits will grateful hearts be found ;
And harvest tide will aye the season be
Of friendly words and harmless jubilee.
The valleys still with festive shouts will ring,
And maidens dance, and rustic minstrels sing ;
The sailor, as he cleaves the Ocean foam,
Will hail the jocund call of harvest home ;
And as the labour ends, and day grows dim,
From hill to hill will roll the harvest hymn ;
While inland, from the Minster's lofty pile
The anthem peals along each vaulted aisle,
And from low walls, which hands less skilful raise,
More simple strains the Lord of Harvest praise.

THE SEA AND THE MINER.

I HAVE no sounding phrases for the Sea,
Its pomp and power and grandeur to declare :
Nay, who, since Byron's mighty line, would dare
With words to measure its immensity ?
'Twas sung of old by greater ev'n than he.
From inland depths where he had wrought for years,
To breathe fresh air and to forget his cares
Went a pale miner forth, from toil set free,
Who of the Sea knew little but the name ;
And when, at last, upon its margin wild
From the wide heather all at once he came,
He stood and gazed in awe ; and then he smiled,
And look'd to Heav'n, and then again survey'd it,
And said but this—' The Sea is His, He made it ! '

THE HARVEST MOON.

1870.

ONCE more the gentle Lady of the Night,
Lovely as Ruth in the glad reaper's sight,
With radiant smile and brow unclouded walks
Amid the nodding sheaves and bending stalks ;
So light her silvery feet move o'er the ground,
They leave no vestige and they make no sound :
Plenty and peace, for that pale bride the dower
That now awaits her in her Island bower.

Such are the scenes in England's harvest fields,
While the broad billows with their azure shields
Guard the rich valleys and the laden shores,
Silent till dawn their busy life restores.

And, as the mild effulgence spreads and falls,
City and village, steeples, towers and halls
Seem all to marble at the touch to change ;
And, far as the enchanted view can range,
Woods, dales, and uplands in the mellow light
Look like a part of fairy-land to-night.

Not many leagues across the glistening sea
Shines the same Moon on nobler scenery,
Where stretch the vineyards and the hills of France
Towards the Rhineland's realm of old romance.
But blood is there ! the country wide is red,
Above the vales lie mountains of the dead,
And o'er the plains spread deep lagoons of blood,
That, if they reach'd, would dye the Ocean's flood.
The spangled skies have caught the purple tinge,
And crimson dews the drooping forests fringe.

Instead of harvest hymns are heard the groans
Of mangled soldiers, and the strange wild tones
Of horses standing maim'd and riderless,
That would their woe and agony express
To their old masters, dead or dying there ;
And from the hamlets, through the sulphurous air,

Burst savage yells, and then the piteous cries
Of women and of homeless children rise ;
While the fierce flame leaps from each vacant roof
As flashes through the street the charger's hoof.
The waggons, plunging in the reeking soil,
Still furrow'd with the cannon's deep recoil,
Are heavy—not with sheaves—but ghastly forms,
That soon will be a harvest for the worms,
While on the ground a larger crop is left
To rot, till tombs like caverns wide are cleft.
Wolves, in men's guise, among the writhing heaps
Prowl, while the ghoul-like hag behind them creeps ;
They clutch their prey when the reveillé peals,
And horsemen almost tread their felon heels.

But hark ! upon the breeze a sound of bells,
And my thought wings to where the Evangel tells
In a far Eastern clime, one winter morn,
Long ages since, the Prince of Peace was born.
His heralds came not with the trumpet's clang,
But his approach ethereal voices sang,
While shepherds rude the strange, sweet music heard,
Yet understood the import of each word—

U

' Glory to God in the highest, Peace on Earth,
Goodwill to men ! '   So was announced his birth,
And the new day flash'd o'er Judæa's hills,
Their spreading cedars and their gushing rills,
And paled the light of sun, and moon, and stars.
Stern soldiers saw it, and forgot their scars ;
And soon new temples rose, and in the aisles
Of minsters loftier than the ancient piles
That chant has peal'd for ages through the world :
But still the blood-stain'd banner is unfurl'd !
And some aver, ' since those blest tidings came,
Just as before, the earth has been the same :
Cain was a tiller of the ground, and now
Thro' lands manured with slaughter'd men we
      plough ;
Red from the fount Life's troubled river ran,
And carnage seems a part of God's own plan ! '

But is it so ?   To say it were to shame
Eternal wisdom, and blaspheme His name.
Ours is the fault, the crime alone is ours !
Our lusts, our passions, and our lawless powers
For ever war against the Will Divine,—
The Love that maketh sun and moon to shine

Alike upon the evil and the good,
The yellow corn-mead and the field of blood,
On Cæsar's palace, and on sheepfolds dim
As those where once was heard the angels' hymn.

Yes, we still hear it as the seasons roll ;
As in the shell the sea, so in the soul
That will but listen breathe its accents yet,
And never will the world the sound forget.
Spring-tide and autumn ratify the pledge :
The feather soon the callow brood will fledge ;
The child becomes the man of care and toil,
And genial Earth from her exhaustless soil
As with a mother's breast his life sustains,
And solaces his patience and his pains.

Ah ! even while I write, the tender plant
It takes so long to raise, should nature grant
That it may live through its first feeble years,
Is treated like a weed the desert rears,
And crush'd and trodden down in gory mire !
Where yesterday, in all their proud attire,
Stood countless ranks like the embattled corn,
White as the forest lilies, strewn and torn

By furious herds, the trampled corses lie :
Happy the dead, the dying glad to die.
Peace ! is it peace ?   Peace is but for the dead,
So calm each sleeps upon his stony bed.

Yet canst thou doubt the message was Divine ?
Believest thou that, while the stars did shine
On that clear night two thousand years nigh past,
The shepherds 'mid their flocks were slumbering
        fast,
And heard that song celestial in a dream ?
And did they only see the meteor's gleam,
And not the radiance of seraphic wings ?
Were all these things but vain imaginings ?
Are all our glorious thoughts but pictured air,
Illusions on the brink of deep despair ?
Are hope and faith and charity mere sound,
And shall no rest for dove-like peace be found ?
And will the better age for ever be
Only a minstrel's passing phantasy ?

Not such my creed.   The morning stars still sing,
In every cloud there is an angel's wing ;

There's not a flower the rugged mountains yield
But teaches like the lilies of the field ;
And all the fruits the shelter'd valleys bear
The same glad tidings from the sky declare ;
And still the blossoms of the heart renew
The bloom of Eden, fresh with heavenly dew.
God careth yet for Earth, and loveth Man
As when the morning of his birth began.
At times His face is darken'd like the sky,
But the frown passes as the clouds roll by :
Wars shake the world as thunders peal thro'
    heaven,
And strong men fall as the gnarl'd oaks are riven ;
But, as 'mid storms the sturdy saplings grew,
So men become by trial brave and true ;
And, like the trees that flourish by the tomb,
The nobler virtues thrive in deepest gloom.

But will it never come, that better age ?
Must war engross the whole historic page ?
And will our journals every day be fill'd
With telling us how thousands have been kill'd ?
Have stalwart arms no nobler work to do
Than cleaving skulls, or driving bayonets through

The soft warm flesh that soon will turn to dust ?
Must we still learn to parry and to thrust ?
Can human skill no greater task achieve
Than fabricating engines that will heave
Bolts deadlier than the dreaded lightnings hurl,
Scattering limbs, brains, and bastions as they whirl ?
Enough for all, in our short span of life,
The common lot of peril, pain, and strife ;
And wide the scope still left on sea and land
For the clear head, stout heart, and ready hand :
Valour is grand, and fortitude sublime,
But doing good is the best work of time.

'Twill come—we know not when, but we believe,
And never yet did trust in God deceive :
'Twill come—or false was the prophetic strain,
'Twill come—or that high Cross was raised in vain :
'Twill come—or martyrs' blood was idly spilt,
And patriots rightly suffer'd for their guilt.
Let eloquence for evermore be dumb,
And mute the lyre for aye, or it will come.
'Twill come—the time when truth shall make all free,
And bind men only in fraternity ;

The reign of law, the faith of filial love,

When every heart in charity will move.

Their spears to ploughshares will they beat, their
    swords

To pruning hooks, as in the ancient words :

Then will be gather'd in o'er all the earth

Harvests of all good things with holy mirth ;

And in the temples nevermore will cease

The echo of the angels' anthem—PEACE !

THE CAPTAIN.

I.

Such was the name the great ship bore,
When with loud cheers from England's shore
She went—but to return no more,
   With her five hundred souls :
And brave Burgoyne was in command,
None worthier on her deck to stand,
As he had proved on that wild strand
   Where the dark Euxine rolls.

II.

Coles too was there, the patient man
Who did her novel structure plan,
Resolute, as when he began,
   To test her daring form :

And eager were the chosen crew
As apt, the seaman's part to do,
To demonstrate the problem true
    In battle or in storm.

III.

One night, when nearing Spain's high coast,
Uprose the gracious, gallant host,
And gave his guests the loyal toast,
    And the bright wine went round :
But from the rock of Finisterre
The light did like a spectre glare,
And the Atlantic breakers there
    Roll'd with a muffled sound.

IV.

Then, as the strong south-west wind blew,
O'er the dark sea the vessel flew,
While, save the trusty Watch, the crew
    Slumber'd and dreamt of home.
Later, a startling call is heard,
Stout arms and prompt obey the word,
But like the wings of wounded bird
    The broad sails flap the foam.

        v

V.

While many slumber still and dream,
The great ship heels upon her beam,
Her lantern now has ceased to gleam,
   And silent is her bell :
No sign—no minute gun—the wave
Booms over the unfathom'd grave
Of hundreds, not less true and brave
   Than at Trafalgar fell !

VI.

The wakeful Admiral counts his fleet,
One lost —one lost ! they all repeat :
Only the wandering mists they meet,
   They hear but Ocean's roar.
Keel after keel above her dips !
A solemn awe pervades the ships,
And prayers are breathed from many lips
   For those that are no more.

VII.

And in her wake that cheerless night
They search'd by their pale lanterns' light,
And still they hoped, when morn rose bright,
   To see her great sail loom :

But in Corcubion's lonely bay
Her shatter'd launch was found that day
With eighteen men—and only they
   Survived to tell her doom !

VIII.

As in an earthquake some great town,
Masts, turrets, hull and men went down ;
But some, from depths where fleets might drown,
   Came to the seething brim :
Most sank again—a few did float,
But fierce the surge and tempest smote,
Yet, with God's help, they reach'd the boat
   By the glimmering starlight dim.

IX.

Keel up the pinnace drifted near,
From which their Captain's voice they hear—
' Keep to your oars, men ! '—firm and clear
   His last command was given :
One grasp'd his hand—the billow broke,
' Save yourself, man ! ' no more he spoke,
And baffled was each oarsman's stroke,
   And wide the boat was driven.

X.

Then one from rocky Cornwall* plied
His oar the helmless boat to guide,
And twelve long hours thro' storm and tide
   He did his task sustain :
But when they reach'd the land at last,
Sighs rose, and briny tears fell fast,
As to that Ocean void and vast
   They turn'd and look'd again.

XI.

The dead, where yon dark waters heave,
In sure and certain hope we leave,
But England for them long will grieve,
   And thousands weep forlorn ;
And while the veering winds shall blow,
And the great ships pass to and fro,
For those beneath that gulf of woe
   The voyager will mourn.

* Charles Tregenna, of Bude.

A SONG FOR SAD MUSIC.

I.

W E are fading away, love,
 Like leaves on the tree ;
We are wearing away, love,
 Like shells by the sea :
On life's wintry shore, love,
 The tide's coming fast,
And we neither can say, love,
 Who'll linger the last.

II.

If one must go first, love,
 Shall I, or will you ?
Have you thought, love, how bitter
 Will be the adieu ?

Oh ! how could we bear, love,
　　To give the last kiss ?
Could we die, love, together,
　　Then death would be bliss.

III.

But that were too selfish,
　　The wish were profane ;
Some doubly would grieve, love,
　　Did neither remain :
It may be for days, love,
　　Or years we shall sever,
But when we next meet, love,
　　It will be for ever.

MARIAN.

I.

Wɪᴛʜ tears the stars glisten,
And hush'd is her lute,
And, while we yet listen,
Her white lips are mute :
The eyes, that beam'd kindly
Till life's painful close,
Now with marble lids blindly
Are seal'd in repose.

II.

But Death's icy fingers
Have now done their worst ;
On the mouth the smile lingers
As when she smiled first

To the smile of her mother,
A babe on the breast ;
And she soon on another
Pure bosom will rest.

III.

Earth will gently receive her,
And be true to our trust,
And God will not leave her
To sleep in the dust :
Though in darkness and sorrow
We part from her now,
She will meet us some morrow
With light on her brow.

August 12, 1874.

THEY ASK FROM ME A FESTIVE SONG.

I.

They ask from me a festive song,
  Some lay of love and youth and beauty,
And chide and marvel that so long
  I sermonize on truth and duty :
They bid me listen to the birds,
  The merry minstrels of the bowers ;
Tell me to choose more sprightly words,
  And wreathe my lute with vernal flowers.

II.

Think ye a chaplet will become
  These silver locks, this brow's deep furrows ?
As veterans march to fife and drum,
  Think ye that I can shake off sorrows,

w

Shoulder my stick, and with a limp
   Keep pace with your elastic measure,
Or, led about by Fancy's imp,
   Be made to caper at your pleasure ?

III.

Too late—too late !   Let me look on,
   And see you trip it—trip it lightly ;
Till from the hall the guests are gone,
   Your eyes than stars will beam more brightly.
When you are joyous I feel gay,
   Your laughter even sets me laughing,
And still I'll sip—if sip I may—
   The sparkling cup which you are quaffing.

IV.

Too soon the garlands will be dead,
   Too soon these fairy scenes will vanish,
And the dark hours we so much dread
   Will all life's dear illusions banish.
Already—do not start—I feel
   A vault-like chillness creeping o'er me,
While, as the chimes of midnight peal,
   A spectral shadow stands before me.

V.

Then ask not for a festive song,

　　Although I'm neither saint nor cynic ;

If old Anacreon may go wrong,

　　Save me from Calvin's lectures clinic !

Bleak Winter will blithe Yule-tide bring,

　　And mistletoe entwine the holly ;

But, gentles, there are blights in Spring,

　　And Mirth is twin of Melancholy.

WELCOME FROM ONE AND ALL.

On the visit at Truro, May 20, 1880, of the Duke and
Duchess of Cornwall with their Sons, when his Royal
Highness laid the Foundation Stone of the Cathedral.

I.

FROM Morwen's breezy headland,
    And Tamar's rippled shore,
And from the West, where underground
    Men hear the Ocean roar,
They speed—they spring in thousands—
    Nor wait for bugle-call,
But swift through Truro's banner'd gates
    Assemble One and All.

II.

Forth from Tregothnan Tower
    The Royal escort comes,
And now the Cornish shout o'erwhelms
    The trumpets and the drums :

Such shout as long since echoed
  In the great Minster's Hall,
Proving how sound are still the hearts
  That beat in One and All.

III.

From One and All warm welcome
  To Cornwall's Duke ; nor less
To the sweet Lady he has brought
  These Isles to grace and bless ;
And so to the fair scions
  No storms, no seas appal,
Types of the hardy Norsemen,
  Welcome from One and All !

IV.

The martial music ceases,
  And now the anthems peal,
For they are here this morning
  The bond of Peace to seal ;
To raise on sure foundations
  A pile that shall not fall,
In which to distant ages
  May worship One and All.

V.

Ay, lay the broad stones truly,
  Ye brethren of the Craft,
And soon in azure Heaven
  The spire will crown the shaft :
A temple of the Eternal,
  Though mortals build the wall ;
And to the Architect Supreme
  Sing praises, One and All !

THE PLAINT OF MORWENSTOW.

I.

' WHY bring they not his body back to me ? '
  A cry was heard along Morwenna's strand ;
' Far from his home near the deep Severn Sea,
  Why was he buried by a stranger's hand ? '

II.

Yes—if their purpose was to keep his soul,
  Why not to Cornish arms his bier entrust ;
So that his own Church-bells for him might toll,
  And Cornwall's tears be sprinkled on his dust ?

III.

His heart was here, whatever they may think,
  And will in Cornish granite be inurn'd
When spires and towers beneath the ground shall sink,
  And till these rocks have into ashes turn'd.

IV.

His faith, some say, he changed, or long conceal'd,
　　Yet happily was not left in Death's dark night
' Unhousell'd, disappointed, unancled,'
　　But soothed and bless'd with every Catholic rite.

V.

And Catholic he was in the true sense,
　　And ever had been, from the distant hour
When light first beam'd on his intelligence,
　　And in the field he cull'd the earliest flower.

VI.

He heard a hymn in every running brook,
　　And, when a boy he reach'd the billow's marge,
The Ocean spread before him as a book
　　In which the word of God was written large.

VII.

Each mountain was for him a giant stair
　　To Heav'n's high altar, and the azure dome
A temple of the Eternal ; built in air,
　　Yet like to outlast the piles of Thebes and Rome.

VIII.

Hierophant of Nature, he became

A Christian Priest, devoted and sincere ;

And was a Clerk in learning as in name,

Whose eloquence could charm the dullest ear.

IX.

He loved to stand upon the ancient ways,

And walk therein, at mouldering shrines would kneel,

Revered the saintly men of other days,

And hurl'd keen gibes at Puritanic zeal.

X.

Was he High Church ?   What's that to you or me ?

A Ritualist ?   Yes—if the word will scan ;

His forms and modes we heed not, sure that he

When he became a priest remain'd a man.

XI.

Liberal he was on just one pound a day,

Wide open to each stranger lay his door,

He ran to help the sufferer by the way,

And knew by heart the ' annals of the poor.'

x

XII.

That he was brave the white-hair'd cragsmen tell
  Round all the coast from Hartland to Pentire ;
And shipwreck'd mariners remember well
  How grand he look'd when flash'd the beacon-fire.

XIII.

As down the cliff he rush'd against the gale,
  Well might he seem the Angel of the Storm ;
While his deep voice the stranded bark would hail,
  His strong arm stretch to save some gasping form.

XIV.

But other fame he earn'd, for which the bard
  Devotes long days and passes sleepless nights ;
Expecting soon or late the high reward
  Which amply for each mental pain requites.

XV.

And that he had the gift of poesy
  Was proved, and some the hour may still recal,
When in his vision of bright Italy
  He saw the death-cloud on Pompeii fall.

XVI.

Of Genoveva in her forest cave,
  Abandon'd on the banks of the broad Rhine,
Where to her babe the doe its udder gave,
  He told in many a sweet and plaintive line.

XVII.

But o'er the scenes that lie 'twixt Bude and Boss
  His fancy hover'd like a sea-bird's wing,
From Nectan's foaming Kieve and fringe of moss
  To Dupath's stream, and Tamar's rushy spring.

XVIII.

To bolder themes at times he struck the chords,
  Of Arthur and the Holy Quest he sang,
Trelawny's name inspired his noblest words,
  And Grenville's stirr'd him like a trumpet's clang.

XIX.

With the great combat of the rocks and waves
  His lyre resounds, as Ocean in the shell,
And in his lay from their unfathom'd caves
  The long-lost bells of Bottreaux hourly knell.

XX.

When falls Tintagel's tower, its solemn chime
  In Hawker's rhythm will echo on the blast,
And still repeat ' Come to thy God in time ! '
  And say to each ' Come to thy God at last ! '

XXI.

He heard and went : but where his dust should sleep,
  Tears on a vacant sepulchre are shed ;
And still the cry comes from Morwenna's steep,
  Complaining that they bring not home the dead.

XXII.

The seabirds miss him on the headland's verge,
  And wailing seek their guardian 'mong these graves ;
And to the cavern'd shore's Æolian dirge
  Succeeds the ' De profundis' of the waves.

XXIII.

Rest where he may, this place is hallow'd ground :
  Genius, Love, Duty, tried by crucial pain,
Here in one noble human mould were found,
  The secrets of his soul with God remain.

LANHYDROCK.

In memory of the Right Hon. Thomas James Lord
Robartes, of Lanhydrock and Truro, who died March 9,
1882; and of Juliana, his wife, who died April 12, 1881.

I.

A CLOUD roll'd from the East, and with a roar
    Down through Restormel forest rush'd the gale
Like lion from its lair ; and ne'er before
    Did gale more fierce invade Fowey's wooded vale :
The rooks rose up in flocks to the dark heaven,
And seamews shrill'd, from creek and headland driven.

II.

And, when it near'd Lanhydrock's still domain,
    Upon the lightning's wings the tempest flew,
With thunders which the torrs flung back again ;
    Then, sweeping over glade and avenue,
On many an ancient stem it left its mark,
While with young budding boughs it strew'd the park.

III.

The agèd inmates from their shelter'd hall
 View'd unalarm'd the approach of that great storm,
For time had not yet shaken roof or wall ;
 And when they saw the impending cloud's black form,
And heard the blast pealing at their own gate,
Suspected not the harbinger of Fate.

IV.

Here, as to their declining years was fit,
 They did in undisturb'd seclusion rest,
Far from the world, but not forgetting it,
 And ever welcome was the casual guest ;
And all who came remember'd long the day
It was their privilege in that home to stay.

V.

Its owner on the stage of public life
 Had play'd a patriot's part most manfully ;
He loath'd the quirks and brawls of party strife,
 And to the cause of truth and liberty
Through all his years was faithful to the last,
As his own kin had proved in ages past.

VI.

Religion here had found a calm retreat,

   And daily rose the sound of household prayer,

While Charity went forth with silent feet

   To seek for those for whom but few would care ;

Or with veil'd hands did as a trust dispense

The garner'd wealth in large beneficence.

VII.

The master had some ways which now look strange :

   The horses that had ceased to serve his need

Were with the kine left free his park to range ;

   Battue and coursing did not suit his creed ;

This his belief, that God regardeth all,

And not unheeded shall one sparrow fall.

VIII.

And now it seems but yesterday that here

   Guests from each Parish West of Tamar's tide

Gather'd, to greet him once more with a cheer,

   And welcome home the son and his young bride ;

And, when to thank the guests the father spoke,

Words from his heart did louder cheers evoke.

IX.

A season follow'd of serene content,
  Then children came and climb'd the grandsire's knee,
Or to the arms of his dear helpmate went,
  And to her bosom clung instinctively ;
Minding her of her own maternal bliss
As with their rosebud lips they met her kiss.

X.

But ere the storm, which spared not flower or leaf,
  Those tenderlings with many a fond caress
Had from Lanhydrock gone ; their sojourn brief,
  But leaving memories of pure happiness.
Alas ! one who went with them to the door,
And linger'd there, would never see them more.

XI.

'Gainst the closed portal soon the furious blast
  Swung like a sledge, and rapid volleys hurl'd
On the embattled walls that still stood fast :
  But suddenly from the tall chimneys whirl'd
Dense clouds of smoke, with flakes of sulphurous fire,
Each moment spreading, mounting high and higher.

XII.

The flakes burst into flames, and then the cry
  Which thrills the bravest thro' each chamber rang,
' Fire ! '—' Fire ! ' and up into the lurid sky
  From burning roofs and blazing rafters sprang
Columns of flame, which from the mountains hoar
Like ancient beacons flash'd to Ocean's shore.

XIII.

And instantly, from mansion, grange, and cot,
  From town and citadel, mine, forge and plough
Men hasten'd, who had not the ways forgot
  That to Lanhydrock lead ; where, under bough
Of beech or oak they oft had shelter found,
Or met the man they loved on his own ground.

XIV.

But could they save the Hall ?   Not till the Sun
  Went down, tho' they had work'd with right goodwill,
And all that strength, skill, courage could, was done,
  The fire was quell'd ; and like a furnace still,
Pent in the roofless walls the red heat glared,
Threatening destruction to the part still spared.

Y

XV.

Then from beneath the antique gallery
  With grateful hearts the agèd inmates came,
Nor fail'd to thank the people audibly,
  For rich and poor that day were all the same :
But not till they look'd back and bade farewell,
And saw once more their ruin'd home, tears fell.

XVI.

The elder bore up like a Christian man,
  And his dear lady with apt words consoled ;
And when, as their lorn pilgrimage began,
  They did again their ancient Church behold,
Unscathed from porch to pinnacle, she smiled,
And that sweet thought their dreary way beguiled.

XVII.

Hard for that lady, hard the shock to bear,
  So frail, so wan, who had survived life's term ;
And though her dearest did her sorrow share,
  And gave her comfort, in her breast the germ
Of death was planted, and on the eighth day
From that dread night her spirit pass'd away.

XVIII.

As o'er the woodland knell'd the plaintive bell,

Up the long avenue the funeral moved

To the grey Tower that overlooks the dell ;

The orphans she had fed and train'd and loved

About her dust as if 'twere living clung,

And round her bier her favourite hymns were sung.

XIX.

When ceased the solemn service, wreaths of flowers,

Types of the virtues that adorn'd her breast,

Were on the coffin placed ; some from the bowers

Cultured by her own hand ; among the rest

Were many that in cottage gardens grew,

Proofs that the poor have feeling hearts and true.

XX.

That death to the survivor was the shock

Which tried his piety and fortitude ;

Though as he watch'd, like shepherd the young flock,

The children his parental joys renew'd ;

While filial love did his sore pangs assuage,

And friendship cheer'd the deepening gloom of age.

XXI.

Before that sad and fatal year roll'd round
   The mourner sicken'd—sicken'd as for death,
And then in her 'a ministering angel' found
   Who not long since came with her bridal wreath
Still fresh on her fair brow, that sunny day
When with festoons the battlements were gay.

XXII.

But the last scene soon closed—'the old man' died,
   Far from the Hall, which from its ashes then
Was rising fast ; far from the hill's green side
   He paced so often ; far from glade and glen,
From dale and river, and from ocean-strand,
And all that knit him to his fatherland.

XXIII.

And, as he wish'd, they brought his body home,
   To rest, as he had long'd, by the dear dead,
Left sleeping lonely in her recent tomb ;
   And when reopen'd was the wall which led
To the dark vault, the wither'd flowers that wreathed
Her coffin still a hallow'd fragrance breathed.

XXIV.

Then, as the bell repeated its sad call,

From many a tower a knell responsive came ;

All Cornwall mourn'd—mourn'd for him One and All ;

And in the distant aftertimes his name

Will be remember'd here, and like a star

It will diffuse its light benignant far.

XXV.

His name will to his son and lineage be

Their best bequest, an heirloom to be worn

On their own breasts, a quickening memory,

To be through life as their escutcheon borne

And by like deeds upheld, and then again

Transmitted without flaw and without stain.

AN EPITAPH.

THE man whose dust rests in this nook of Earth
By rank was noble, nobler still by worth,
Gave none offence, upon no creature trod,
Did right, loved mercy, humbly walk'd with God,
And, when his steps to the dark vale drew near,
Trusted in God, and did no evil fear.

March, 1882.

NOTES.

———

Among the authorities cited in these notes are the Manuscript of Hals' Parochial History of Cornwall, Carew's Survey of Cornwall, Whitaker's Cathedral of Cornwall, Dr. Borlase's Antiquities, the Rev. R. Polwhele's Cornwall, Messrs. Lysons' Cornwall, S. C. Gilbert's Cornwall, Davies Gilbert's Cornwall, and Sir John Maclean's History of Trigg Minor.

The manuscript of Hals, which is now in the British Museum, was given to me by the widow of Richard Taunton of Truro, M.D., and had been for some time in the possession of her father, the Rev. John Whitaker, author of the Cathedral of Cornwall. It is deficient of several parishes, probably from want of care on the part of the printer to whom it was entrusted for publication. Mr. Lysons had a copy of it on vellum, which on the sale of his books was purchased by the then Earl of Aylesford. That copy does not contain the missing parishes. It was from the defective manuscript that Mr. Davies Gilbert made the extracts which appear in his book under the name of Hals. He omits most of the digressions, and much of the family gossip in which the old writer indulged.

THE VOYAGE OF ARUNDEL.

The subject of this poem was suggested by the following passage from 'A Fortnight in Kerry,' published in Fraser's Magazine for April, 1870, which bore the initials of the Editor, Mr. Froude. ' From the description given of the scene by Walsingham the historian, Scariff is not improbably the place where a Cornish knight in the time of the Second Richard came to a deserved and terrible end. It was a very bad time in England. Religion and society were disorganised ; and the savage passions of men, released from their natural restraints, boiled over in lawlessness and crime. Sir John Arundel, a gentleman of some distinction, had gathered together a party of wild youths to make an expedition to Ireland. He was wind-bound either at Penzance or St. Ives ; and being in uneasy quarters, or the time hanging heavy on his hands, he requested hospitality from the abbess of a neighbouring nunnery. The abbess, horrified at the prospect of entertaining such unruly guests, begged him to excuse her. But neither excuses nor prayers availed. Arundel and his companions took possession of the convent, which they made the scene of unrestrained and frightful debauchery. The sisters were sacrificed to their appetites, and when the weather changed were carried off to the ship and compelled to accompany their violators. As they neared the Irish Coast the gale increased in its fury. Superstition is the inseparable companion of cowardice and cruelty, and the wretched women were flung overboard to propitiate the demon of the storm. "Approbatum est non esse curæ Deis securitatem nostram, esse ultionem." If Providence did not interfere to save the honour or the lives of the nuns, at the least it avenged their fate. The ship drove before the south-wester, helpless as a disabled wreck. She was hurled on Scariff, or probably on Cape Clear, and was broken instantly to pieces. A handful of half drowned wretches were saved by the inhabitants to relate their horrible tale. Arundel himself, being a powerful swimmer, had struggled upon the rocks alive, but he was caught by a returning wave before he could climb beyond its reach, and he was whirled away in the boiling foam.'

After reading this extract, I was enabled, through the kindness of the late Rev. J. J. Wilkinson of Lanteglos, formerly a Fellow of Queen's College, Oxford, to refer to the old edition of Walsingham's history in the Library of that College, and I have since procured the edition by Mr. Riley of the Inner Temple, published under the direction of the Master of the Rolls. Walsingham does not state the port in England from which the expedition first sailed, or that it reached the Cornish shore, but he describes it as having been fitted out to assist the Duke of Brittany. He details the atrocities referred to by Mr. Froude, but points to the companions of Sir John Arundel as the chief criminals, and leaves it to be inferred that the knight was an accessary, if not a principal.

According to the old chronicler the outrages were committed on the nuns, and also on the ladies who resided in the Abbey for protection, the novices, and the young persons placed there for education. The abduction of the women is, however, given with the qualifying expressions 'quæ vi vel sponte in naves ascenderant.' As to the charge of throwing them overboard to lighten the vessels in the great storm, I have preferred to indicate rather than to affirm the fact, and to leave room for the charitable supposition that they were washed off the deck into the

z

sea. In other particulars I have relied on Walsingham's narrative, which is so precise and circumstantial as to leave little doubt that it is substantially true.

He says that Arundel permitted the crews to plunder the neighbourhood ; that they committed sacrilege in the church ; that they carried off not only women from the Abbey, but also a newly married woman ; and that they were excommunicated by the priest. But he records to the honour of Sir Hugh Calverley and Sir Thomas Percy, who belonged to the expedition, that they remonstrated, and desired to make amends to the people there for the injuries inflicted on them.

He then tells how they set sail, and were overtaken by a tempest, and adapts passages from the Æneid to describe its violence, adding the terror of a supernatural vision which haunted Arundel's ship ; and describes the throwing of the women into the sea and the approach to the Irish coast in the following passage :—

'Idcirco, quid inter hæc agerent dubitabant, cum hinc ventis et procellis, illinc fluctibus et fœminarum clamoribus, urgerentur. Tentavit ergo primo alleviare vasa, projicientes vilia, dehinc quæque pretiosa, si forte vel sic eis exsurgeret spes salutis. Sed cum ita non minus desperationem, said potius augeri cernerent, refundunt causas infortuníii in ipsas fœminas, ac, in spiritu furoris, eisdem manibus quibus ante illas blande attractaverant, eisdem brachiis quibus eas libidinose demulserant, arreptas in mare projiciunt ; ad numerum, ut fertur, sexaginta fœminarum, piscibus et marinis belluis devorandas. Sed ita quidem non cessavit tempestas, sed excrevit per amplius, ut cunctis omnem spem adimeret mortis pericula evadendi. Cumque diebus aliquot atque noctibus, non tantum in mortis periculo quantum in mortis faucibus, non sine trepidatione maxima transegissent, tandem vidit quoddam littus, et quandam insulam, in regione Hiberniæ, circa littus illud in fluctibus marinis sitam ; unde momentaneo gaudio perfusus, Dominus Johannes Arundelle mox jubet ut nautæ se transferant ad littus illud, si forte eis terram contingere donaretur.'

Walsingham concludes with the shipwreck on the coast of Ireland, and the drowning of Arundel, his brave master De Rust, his esquire Musard, and others of rank. Some of the shipwrecked persons were rescued by the Irish, and the body of Arundel was found three days after the wreck, and buried in an abbey in Ireland. Twenty-five other ships were lost in the same storm.

Froissart states that the expedition sailed from Southampton for Brittany, that the ships were driven by stress of weather to the Cornish shore, and that they were afterwards lost on the coast of Ireland. He speaks of Arundel as a valiant and enterprising knight, and makes 'no' mention of the atrocities detailed by Walsingham. He spells the name as I have done, and as Froissart and Carew spell it, with a single final l, but the Cornish historians usually spell the name as Arundell. The knight was probably descended from one of the branches of the family of Arundell, of which Lord Arundell of Wardour is now the head.

In designating the Cornish port or ports where the fleet anchored, and the site of the Abbey, I have partly followed the suggestions of Mr. Froude, availing myself of the opportunity of introducing local scenes. In my endeavour to trace the site of an Abbey at Penzance and at St. Ives, I found at Penzance a street still called Abbey Street, but, as regards Saint Ives, I can only rely on the statements of Borlase and Lysons that in their times

there were remains of religious edifices there. The place
was formerly called Porth-Ia, after the religious woman
mentioned in ' Oliver's Monasticon,' p. 439. He says
Saint Hya, or Hia, otherwise Ia or Ya, was the parochial
saint, and that she was an Irish Virgin who died at Hayle
in Cornwall, about the middle of the fifth century. At
Hayle, therefore, if not at or near St. Ives, there may
have been a religious house in the time of Arundel.
Camden speaks of Saint Ia as the guardian of the parish
of St. Ives, and says she was an Irishwoman that preached
the gospel in that place. Tonkin writes:—' On the
peninsula, north of St. Ives, stand the ruins of an old
chapel wherein God was duly worshipped by our ancestors, the Britons, before the Church at St. Ives was erected
or endowed.'

Respecting the religious edifices on St. Michael's
Mount and its history from remote times, Mr. Davies
Gilbert has in his Parochial History collected from Hals,
Tonkin, Whitaker, and other sources, much information.
Leland and Hals agree there were two churches or
chapels on the summit of the Mount, that on the south
being the Chapel of Saint Michael, that on the east the
Chapel of Saint Mary. Whitaker says there was for a
considerable period a nunnery there, as well as a monastery; and that when the Mount was garrisoned with
soldiers, the nuns abandoned their cells, but the monks
remained there from the period of Edward the Confessor
till the reign of Henry the Fifth.

After 1642 the Mount became the property of Sir John
Basset, and in 1660 it passed to Sir John St. Aubyn, and
after possession by six Sir John St. Aubyns in succession
it came to the late Sir Edward St. Aubyn, and is now held
by his son Sir John St. Aubyn, M.P. for West Cornwall.

The old church of the Benedictines, which is now the chapel of the mansion, forms with its tower the central mass of the buildings on the Mount. The other monastic buildings, which had become ruinous in the latter part of the last century, were replaced by the Sir John St. Aubyn of that time with several rooms that retain their Georgian fittings. But under the present Baronet great additions have been made by the professional skill of his relative, Mr. P. S. St. Aubyn, without impairing the ancient outline; and the place, which has been celebrated in romance and song for ages, will continue to be regarded as the gem of the Western shores.

ST. GURON.

THE clergyman referred to in the first stanza, the late Rev. John Wallis, was for forty-nine years Vicar of St. Petrock's, Bodmin. Cornwall is indebted to him for two valuable works, the Bodmin Register and the Cornwall Register.

The ancient missionary, called St. Guron, is mentioned by Whitaker in the 'Cathedral of Cornwall.' He says:—'Down to the days of Athelstan, Bodmin had no existence as a town, not even as a village, but was merely a hermitage. Athelstan, say those best authorities that we can have, the ancient charters of donations, founded a monastery at Bodmin, in a valley where St. Guron, the patron saint and denominator of the parish of Goran, near

Mevagissey, was living solitarily in a small hut which he
left and resigned to St. Petrock.* This appears, from its
position in the valley, to have been upon the site of the
present churchyard ; and it is pleasing to contemplate, in
the glass of history, the area of a town once the ground of
a hermitage. . . . . What attracted St. Guron to
the ground, in addition to the general woodiness and
general solitariness of it, was that perpetual, that necessary accompaniment of a saint's hermitage in our island,
a fine fountain of water. This remains to the present
moment, at the western end of the church, and so points
out the immediate site of the hermitage with the strictest
precision. . . . . This ran waste between the hills,
till it engaged his notice, and invited the residence of St.
Guron in the end of the fifth century, or at the beginning
of the sixth, as St. Petrock came into Cornwall in 518.'

SAINTS.

For an account of the multiplication of Saints, see
Milman's ' Latin Christianity,' vol. ix, pp. 76 and 82.

He says :—' The East and the West vied with each
other in their fertility. Popular admiration for some time
enjoyed, unchecked, the privilege of canonisation, A
Saint was a Saint, as it were by acclamation ; and this
acclamation might have been uttered in the rudest times,
as during the Merovingian Rule in France ; or, within a
very limited sphere, as among our Anglo-Saxon ancestors,

* Leland's Coll. i., 75. ' In valle ubi S. Guronus fuit solitarie
degens in parvo tugurio, quod relinquens tradidit S. Petroco.'

so many of whose Saints were contemptuously rejected by the Norman Conqueror. Saints at length multiplying thus beyond measure, the Pope assumed the prerogative of advancing to the successive ranks of Beatitude and Sanctity.'

In proof of the corruption in the appellations of Saints, I will cite but three instances. St. Enodock is commonly called 'Sinkineddy,' and Mevagissey or Menaguisey is, according to Carew, derived from the titular Saints of the place, St. Meny and St. Issey. 'Simonward' is a marvellous corruption of St. Breward. It is said by some that the name of a famous brewer of beer in that district, Simon Ward, has been substituted for that of the Saint.

THE FRIAR'S BONE.

THE bone which was the text for these verses is believed to have been a friar's bone, having been found in the burial ground appurtenant to the 'place of Grey Freres' mentioned by Leland, 'on the south side of Bodmyne Towne.'

Hals says, ' above all others, there is still extant in this town the stately church of the Franciscan Friars, dedicated to St. Nicholas, and their cells consisting of one roof twenty cloth-yards high and fifty long, with the stone windows, admirable for height, breadth, and workmanship; which, after the dissolution of their house and order by King Henry the Eighth, the justices of the peace for this county appointed for a house of correction for such vagrant and idle persons as the same afforded, by the name of the Friary and Shire-Hall; which the towns-

men taking notice of soon after converted or profaned it
further to a common market-house, for selling corn, wool
and other commodities weekly ; yea, and within the same
is kept yearly several fairs for selling all sorts of merchan-
dize, the altars being pulled down, and in the churchyard,
or burial-place, a fair of cattle ! It also lately made the
tribunal or hall for the judges of assize yearly, and the
justices of the peace in their sessions, and is undoubtedly,
except Westminster Hall, the fairest and best in England.'

The larger hall, which was sometimes called the Refectory, is believed by Sir John Maclean to have been the
Friary church. It was 150 feet in length and 60 feet
high, and had a fine east window of Second pointed work.
He adds, with the indignation of an inveterate anti-
quarian, ' the building was ruthlessly destroyed to make
room for the new Assize Courts, (in 1837,) the walls being
thrown down without even removing the tracery of the
windows. A skeleton was discovered inclosed in a tomb in
the masonry of the wall, and many graves and vaults
were found under the floor.' Sir Hugh and Sir Thomas
Peverille were buried in the church. William de London,
a merchant of the great city, and who is described as the
tailor of Henry III., began the Friary, and Edmund Earl
of Cornwall augmented it.

At the dissolution, the inmates of the Friary and those
of the Priory at Bodmin were summarily expelled.
The buildings and lands of the Friary were soon after
transferred to the Corporation of that town, and the
buildings of the Priory were for the most part demolished,
and the ground on which they stood and some of the
adjacent lands belonging to them were conveyed to the
Rev. Thomas Sternhold, one of the authors of the old
version of Psalms.

If the Franciscans in other parts of England deserved the invectives of Matthew Paris, Wyclyffe, and others, there is no record or tradition which impeaches the grey friars of Bodmin. But proofs are extant that peace and prosperity did not always prevail in the Priory. Complaints were from time to time made by the Mayor, burgesses, and towns folk of Bodmin against the Priory, and on their petition to Lord Cromwell in 1539 a commission was granted by the King to——Edgcumbe, knight, Sir John Chamonde, John Arundell, Humfrey Predyaux and Thomas Treffry, Esqs., to inquire into alleged grievances. These documents and the subsequent proceedings are set out in Mr. Wallis's book.

More important, as showing the internal condition of the Priory, is the letter addressed by the last Prior, Thomas Wandsworth, to Mr. Loke of London, printed among the letters relating to the suppression of the monasteries collected by Mr. Wright, and published by the Camden Society in 1843. The following is a copy :—

'Syr,—I am sore disquieted with a set of unthryfty chanons, my convent and their berars, which of longe contynuans, have lyvyd unthriftili and agane the gode order of religyon, to the great sklaundre of the same as all the contrey can telle. For the reformacyon thereof, the buschope yn hys late visitacyon gave certayne and dyvers injunctions, commandyng me straytle to see observyd and kept, which are noo harder thane ower owne rule and profession byndis us, and as alle other relygyus men use and observe where gode relygioun is observyd and and kept ; wherewith they be sore grevid, and yntend the most parte of them to depart with capacitise without my concent and wylle, and won of them hath purchesyd a capacyte the last terme without my lycence, which is

A 2

agcne the wordes of his capacite, wherefore I have restray-
nyd his departyng, for no gret los that I should have of
hym, but for yl exemple to othere ; for yf I should suffer
this man to depart yn this maner, I shall have never a
chanon to byde with me.

'From Bodmyn, 25 May, by your owne for ever,

'Thomas, priour there.'

' *To the right worshipfull*
Master W. Loke, mercer,
dwellyng yn Chepscyde, at
the synge of the Padlok,
this be dd. with spede.'

In the preface to the collection Mr. Wright says,
' These letters tell their own tale. They throw a light on
the history of a great event which changed the face of
society in our island, an event which I regard as the
greatest blessing conferred by Providence on this country
since the first introduction of the Reformation.' That
many still concur in that opinion has been testified in the
year 1884 by the commemoration of the Quincentennary
of Wyclyffe, whose translation of the Bible still continues his best monument; and by the unveiling in the
gardens of the Thames Embankment of the statue of
Tyndale, who, having been obliged to quit England to
complete his translation of the New Testament, was
arrested at Antwerp, and tried, condemned, strangled and
burnt at Augsburgh in 1536. The prophetic words he
uttered when he began his translation, that if God spared
his life he would ere many years cause the boy at the
plough to know the Scriptures, have been verified in
every parish from the Orkneys to the Land's End.

While sentimentalising on the desolation of the past,
it may be well to recall some of the dark realities of his-

tory, and to remember that all was not bright and fair which is now enveloped with the dust and mist of ages. Fuller, referring to the suppression of the monasteries, calls it ' the great dissolution or judgment day of the world of abbeyes whose magnificent ruines may lesson the beholder that it is not the firmnesse of the stone nor fastnesse of the morter maketh strong walles, but the integritie of the inhabitants.'

Of the Bodmin Friary almost the only remains are the dilapidated buildings to the west of the Assize Courts, masked with a semi-Gothic front, one part having been converted into a schoolroom, and the rest being used for storing market hurdles and the arms and ammunition of Volunteers.

THE LADY OF PLACE.

HALS gives a long account of the attack on Fowey by the Lord Pomier and other Normans in 1457, and Carew says ' the Lord Pomier, a Norman, encouraged by the civill warres, wherewith our realm was then distressed, furnished a navy within the river of Sayne, and with the same in the night burned a part of Foy, and other houses confyning: but upon approch of the countryes forces, raised the next day by the sherife, he made speed away to his ships, and with his ships to his home.'

Leland says ' the Frenchmen diverse times assailed this town, and last, most notably, about Henry the VI. time, when the wife of Thomas Trewry the 2, with the men, repelled the French out of her house in her house-bandes absence. Whereupon, Thomas Trewry builded a

right fair and stronge embatelid tower in his house, and
embateling all the walles of the house, in a maner
made it a castelle.'

On entering the grounds of Place from the churchyard,
an arched doorway is seen, over which there is a statue in
a niche with this inscription under it :—

'Elizabeth, the wife of Thomas Treffry, the second,
(Junr.) with her men repelled the ffrench out of her
house, during her husband's absence, in July 1457.'

GALLANTS OF FOWEY.

THE freebooting spirit of some of the sailors of Fowey in
the old times was not peculiar to them, and they were no
worse than the maritime population of other places in
England and on the Continent. Piracy more or less prevailed in our seas down to the time of the Stuarts, when
Sir John Eliot, then Vice-Admiral of the West, after
much stratagem, succeeded in capturing the notorious sea-
robber, Captain Nutt, in Torbay. That Prince of English
Corsairs had a fleet of some twenty-five ships under his
command; and he, by some means, obtained the protection of powerful persons about the Court, so that he was
enabled to carry on his lawless expeditions with impunity
for many years.

The Fowey men having grown rich by lawful prizes in
war and by merchandise ' hereupon,' in the quaint language of Carew, ' a full purse begetting a stout stomach,
our Foyers took heart at grasse, and refused to vaile their
bonets,' or to dip their flag, in passing near Rye or Winchelsea; but they had to do battle with the sturdy

people there for their haughtiness, and having proved themselves the better men, they were thenceforth, according to Carew, called 'Gallants of Fowey,' He describes how their spirits were afterwards humbled by a Flemish ship of war, which took one of their full laden barges, and slaughtered 'all the saylors, one onely boy excepted; and not long after our Fowey Gallants, unable to beare a lowe sayle, in their fresh gayle of fortune, began to skum the seas with their often piracies.'

Some troubles followed, in the course of which one of their townsmen, Harrington, was executed by the Commissioners of Edward the Fourth, which had such an effect on them, that they for ages pursued ther lawful vocation as merchants and sailors; and ultimately Carew was enabled to say ' They of late yeres doe more and more aspire to a great amendment of their former defects.'

COTEHELE—BODRIGAN.

Hals states that Henry Trenoweth, or Bodrigan, 'was knighted by Edward IV. or Richard III., by the name of Sir Henry Bodrigan; who siding with King Richard at the battle of Bosworth Field, he was with many others attainted of treason against Henry VII.; and in order to shun justice, he made his escape after the battle aforesaid, and secretly repaired to this place (his castle in Gorun), where he was kept close for a season, but not so private but King Henry's officers got notice thereof, and at an appointed time beset the same in quest of him; which he understanding, by a back door fled from thence, and ran down the hills to the sea-cliff near the same, the officer pursuing so quick after him that he could not possibly make his escape. As soon, therefore, as he came to the cliff, about a hundred feet high, he leaped down into the sea, upon the little grassy island there, without much hurt or damage; whence instantly a boat, which he had prepared in the cove, attended him there, which transported him to a ship which carried him to France, which astonishing fact and place is to this day known and remembered by the name of Bodrigan's Leap or Jump. But notwithstanding his own escape beyond the seas, his lordship and his whole estate were forfeited and seized by King Henry VII. for attainder of treason; and the greatest part thereof he settled on Sir Richard Edgcumb and his heirs for ever, whose posterity is still in possession thereof. This Sir Richard Edgcumb not long before, on suspicion of being confederated with the Earl of Richmond against King Richard III. (as tradition saith), was shrewdly sought after and pursued by means of this very Henry Bodrigan, in order to be taken into custody, who from his house at Cothele made also a wonderful escape thence, and got into France to the Earl of Richmond : so unavoidable a thing is fortune or destiny.'

On these incidents Davies Gilbert observes that Sir Henry having escaped into Cornwall, he endeavoured to defend his house against Edgcumbe and Trevanion, who, in despoiling him, did no more than he would have done; or than what he actually did against Sir Richard Edgcumbe a few years before at Cothele. Such are the effects of Civil Wars, when, in the words of Gray,

> ' Long years of havoc hold their destined course,
> And through the kindred squadrons mow their way.'

In the notes to Polwhele's Cornwall, book 4th, will be

found extracts from various authorities respecting Sir Richard Edgcumbe and his descendants. He was distinguished not only as a soldier but as a statesman; he became comptroller of Henry the Seventh's household, and a member of the privy council; and he was employed in several embassies. Another of the same name in the reign of Mary is described by Carew as eminent for knowledge, courtesy, and liberality, and he was commonly called ' the good old Knight of the Castle.' The present Earl of Mount Edgcumbe, now Lord Lieutenant of Cornwall, is a lineal descendant of the first Sir Richard Edgcumbe, and it is no flattery of his lordship to say that, with the large possessions, he inherits the noble qualities of his ancestors.

Of Sir Henry Bodrigan's movements after the battle of Bosworth Field, which was fought in August, 1485, the accounts are contradictory; though they agree that he escaped from his castle as described by Hals and others. One account states that he joined the insurrection headed by the Earl of Lincoln in favour of Lambert Simnel, and that he was slain, as well as the Earl, at the battle of Stoke in June, 1486. Another account is that he escaped from that battle into Cornwall, and in the February following a writ was issued to Sir Richard Edgcumbe to ar-arrest him and others implicated in that insurrection; and, after a skirmish on the place called the ' dismal moor,' he escaped by leaping into the sea from the cliff at Gorran which is still pointed out as the spot of Bodrigan's Leap. Sir John Maclean in his book of Trigg Minor, referring to the family of Bodrigan in connection with their property in the parish of Endellion, adopts this view on the authorities he cites. It is believed that Sir Henry Bodrigan afterwards remained in foreign countries till his death, when the name became extinct.

In the ' Antiquities of Cornwall' Dr. Borlase describes the remains of Bodrigan Castle as very extensive, and says there was nothing in the County equal to it for magnificence. He speaks of a chapel which had been converted into a barn, the large hall, and an ancient kitchen with a timber roof; and supposes the architecture to have been of the time of Edward I. All the buildings were pulled down about the year 1786.

Of Cotehele Carew says ' the buildings are ancient, large, strong, and faire, appurtenanced with the necessaries of wood, water, fishing, parks, and mils, with the devotion of (in times past) a rich furnished Chappell, and with the charity of almes-houses for certain poore people whom the owners vsed to releeue. It is reported, and credited thereabouts, how Sir Rich. Edgcumb the elder was driven to hide himself in those his thick woods, which ouerlook the riuer, what time being suspected of fauoring the Earle of Richmond's party, against King R. the 3. He was hotely pursued, and narrowly searched for. Which extremity taught him a sudden policy, to put a stone in his cap, and tumble the same into the water, while these rangers were fast at his heeles, who looking downe after the noyse, and seeing his cap swimming thereon, supposed that he had desperately drowned himself, gave ouer their further hunting, and left him liberty to shift away, and slip over into Brittaine: for a grateful remembrance of which deliuery, hee afterwards builded in the place of his lurking, a Chappell not yet utterly destroyed.'

The Chapel, erected by Sir Richard Edgcumbe as a grateful memorial of his escape from his pursuers, is now, as it has long been, kept with pious care in perfect repair. But another relic of still remoter date, the Chestnut Tree which with its coevals was standing on the bank of the Tamar in view of that escape, went down in the storm of the 26th January, 1884. It measured 36 feet in girth, and a few feet above the ground it branched into three, and each of its giant limbs became the trunk of a lofty tree covered with foliage to the summit; verifying the description in the Faery Queen of the tree

‘ So fair and great, that shadow'd all the ground.’

It is mentioned by the Rev. C. A. Johns in his book of the Forest Trees of Britain, published in 1849, and describing its appearance at that time he says that, though it did not equal some other chestnut trees of great age, it was scarcely less imposing from its not showing symptoms of decay. Of late, however, it had needed the support and protection of chains and bands ; but it continued to the last to be an object of veneration to all visitors, and its loss will be long lamented by many.

THE WHITE ROSE.

LORD BACON, in his Life of Henry VII., while he treats Warbeck as an impostor, and calls him a little cockatrice of a king, writes in terms of admiration and respect of his wife, who was the Lady Catharine Gordon, a daughter of the Earl of Huntley, and a near kinswoman to the King of Scots. He speaks of her as a young virgin of excellent beauty and virtue, and as afterwards having entirely loved her husband, in all fortunes, adding the virtues of a wife to the virtues of her sex. ‘ When she was brought to the King,’ he says, ‘ it was commonly said that the King

B 2

received her not only with compassion, but with affection ;
pity giving more impression to her excellent beauty.
Wherefore comforting her to serve his eye as well as his
fame, he sent her to his queen, to remain with her ; giving
her a very honourable allowance for the support of her
estate, which she enjoyed both during the King's life, and
many years after. The name of the White Rose, which
had been given to her husband falsely, was continued in
common speech to her beauty.'

THE UNGRACIOUS RETURN.

CAREW gives the following account : 'Sir Anthony Kingston, then Prouost Marshall of the King's Armie (temp.
Ed. 6.), hath left his name more memorable than com-
mendable amongst the townsmen, for causing their Maior
to erect a gallows before his owne doore, upon which (after
having feasted Sir Anthony) himself was hanged. In
like sort (say they) he trussed vp a miller's man thereby,
for that he presented himself in the other's stead, saying
he could neuer do his master better seruice.

'But men's tongues, readily inclined to the worst
reports, have left out a part of the truth in this tale, that
the rest might carrie the better grace. For Sir Anthony
did nothing herein, as a judge by discretion, but as an
officer by direction ; and besides, hee gave the Maior
sufficient watchwordes of timely warning, and large space
of respite (more than which, in regard to his owne perill,
he could not afford) to shift for safety, if an vneschewable
destiny had not haltered him to that aduancement.'

C. S. Gilbert has another version of the story. 'This

wretch (Sir Anthony Kingston), who was the Provost
Marshall of the King's Army, on his coming to Bodmin,
sent orders to Boyer, the Mayor, who had been rather
active in promoting the insurrection, to cause a gibbet to
be erected in the street, opposite to his own house, by the
next day at noon, letting him know that he would dine
with him, in order to be present at the execution of some
rebels. The unsuspecting Boyer obeyed his command,
provided an entertainment for his guest, and at the time
appointed regaled his visitors, who put about the wine till
the Mayor's spirits were rather exhilarated, when Kingston asked him if the gibbet was ready? Being informed
that it was, Kingston, with a diabolical sneer, ordered him
to be hanged upon it.' Kingston further distinguished
himself by hanging the Portreeve of St. Ives in the
middle of the town; and being himself afterwards implicated in a design to rob the Exchequer, he terminated
his existence by poison.

Hals says of this functionary that he executed martial
law with 'sport and justice.' One of his feats, as told
by that gossiping chronicler, is that he hanged Mr. Mayow
of St. Columb at the tavern sign-post in that town, of
whom tradition saith his crime was not capital; and
therefore his wife was advised by her friends to hasten to
the town after the Marshall and his men, who had him in
custody, and beg his life. Which accordingly she prepared to do, and to render herself the more amiable
petitioner before the Marshall's eyes, this dame spent so
much time in attiring herself and putting on her French
hood, then in fashion, that her husband was put to death
before her arrival!'

THE TIMES OF THE CAVALIERS.

IF the character of Sir Beville Grenville had not been
embalmed in the pages of Clarendon, his memory would
continue to be perpetuated, as it has been for more than
two centuries, by grateful tradition.

The closing passage of Clarendon's account of the battle
of Lansdown is a fitting epitaph for the great Cornishman:—'In this battle, on the King's part, there were
more officers and gentlemen slain, than common men;
and more hurt than slain. That which would have clouded
any victory, and made the loss of others less spoken of,
was the death of Sir Bevil Greenvil (so the historian spells
the name). He was indeed an excellent person, whose
activity, interest, and reputation was the foundation of
what has been done in Cornwall; and his temper and
affections so publick, that no accident which happened
could make any impression in him; and his example
kept others from taking anything ill, or at least seeming
to do so. In a word, a brighter courage, and a gentler
disposition, were never married together to make the most
cheerful and innocent conversation.'

The motives which impelled him so strongly in behalf
of his unfortunate King, are expressed in the following
extract from Sir Beville's letter to Sir John Trelawny,
printed in Lord Nugent's Memoirs of Hampden : —

' I have in many kindes had tryall of y^r noblenes, but in
' none more than in this singular expression of y^r kind care
' and love. I give also y^r excell^t Lady humble thanks for
' respect unto my poore woman, who hath been long a
' faithful much obliged servant of your Ladyes. But, S^r,
' for my journey, it is fixt. I cannot containe myself

' w^{thin} my doores, when the K^g of Eug^s standard waves
' in the field upon so just occasion—the cause being such
' as must make all those that dye in it little inferior to
'martyrs. And, for myne owne, I desire to acquire an
' honest name, or an hon^{ble} grave. I never loved my life
' or ease so much as to shunn such an occasion, wch if I
' should, I were unworthy of the profession I have held,
' or to succede those ances. of mine, who have so many of
' thém, in severall ages, sacrificed their lives for their
' conntry.'

' It was,' Lord Nugent says ' at the most unpromising
period of the King's affairs that the brave Sir Beville
Grenvil declared himself in the field, and in a moment of
general doubt and dismay, first published the commission
of array, and raised troops and occupied a line of posts
in the West. In his native County of Cornwall, which
he had long represented in Parliament, he took his part
as one who, having weighed and resolved with caution,
was now ready to act with determination and effect.
There was no man who had more faithfully done his duty
in the House of Commons against the arbitrary measures
of the King. He had earnestly associated himself with
the reformers of abuses, and, personally and politically
attached to Sir John Eliot, had joined in the remonstran-
ces on his commitment. But Sir Beville seems never to
have contemplated the possibility of any justification in
any case for a subject resisting a sovereign in arms, and to
have considered the weapons of war as to be used by a
good man at the bidding of his sovereign only, and that
such bidding always makes the use just and glorious.'

He was the grandson of Vice-Admiral Sir Richard
Grenville, the hero of Lord Tennyson's fine ballad ' The
Revenge,' who in his little ship in 1591 sailed forth from

' Flores in the Azores,' and attacked and beat off a Spanish fleet of 53 sail, and then died of his wounds; when his astonished and admiring foes ' sank his body with honour down into the deep.' Sir Beville, not more honoured but more happy in his burial, was brought from his gory bed on Lansdown to lie among his forefathers in the vault in Kilkhampton church. The monument erected there by his eldest son, who was created Earl of Bath, describes him as Sir Beville Granville of Stowe, and Earl of Corbill and Lord of Thorigny and Granville in France and Normandy, and as descended in a direct line from Robert, second son of Rollo Duke of Normandy. Through Jane a granddaughter of Sir Beville, his blood descends to the Duke of Sutherland, the Earl of St. Germans, Lady Louisa Fortescue of Boconnoc, Earl Granville, the Hon. F. Leveson-Gower,* and to other noble connections; and from Grace another granddaughter the line is continued in the Marquis of Bath and others of the Thynne family.

The Cornish property is now held by Francis John eldest son of the late Lord John Thynne, another son of whom, the Rev. Canon Thynne, is now Rector of Kilkhampton, where many of the Grenville race are buried.

In Lord Nugent's Memorials there is an engraving of Sir Beville from a miniature said to have been in the possession of the Rt. Hon. Thomas Granville; and attached to it is an autograph in which the name is spelt ' Bevill Grenvil.'

The same work contains, among other matter relating to the Cornish hero, a copy of the pathetic letter written by Sir John Trelawny, announcing Sir Beville's death to the Lady Grace, his widow.

* M.P. for Bodmin.

Of Sir Beville's retainer, Anthony Payne, there is a long account in C. S. Gilbert's history, with a portrait from the picture by Kneller, which, after lying for a long time as lumber in a farm-house, was purchased by a connoisseur for eight pounds, and afterwards fetched no less a sum than eight hundred pounds. On C. S. Gilbert's narrative, and such other information as I could gather, so much of my ballad as alludes to Payne had been composed, when my attention was directed to the account given of him by the late R. S. Hawker of Morwinstow, in his ' Footprints of Former Men in Far Cornwall.' For this work we owe another debt of grateful remembrance to the author of Cornish Ballads and Poems. I would quote the manly and touching letter from Payne to Sir Beville's widow, informing her of the death of her husband at Lansdown, and the noble conduct there of the youth her son,' but that I trust the letter will be read in the ' Footprints ' by many who love the old associations which have made Cornwall memorable among English counties.

In the stanza describing the close of the fight at Lansdown I have introduced, with slight variation, the words which Payne tells us his humane master uttered at Stamford Hill, to check the fury of the Cornish against their vanquished foes—' Halt, men; God will avenge !' And in the last line of another verse I have adapted part of the closing paragraph of the same letter,—' O ! my lady, how shall I ever brook your weeping face ?'

As a set-off against these sentiments, I extract a passage from the account given by Hals of the battle of Stamford Hill :—' The country people hereabout will tell you, that the field aforesaid where the battle was fought, being afterwards tilled to barley, produced sixty bushels of corne, Winchester measure, in every acar: the fertility whereof is ascribed to the virtue the land received from the blood and ordure of slain men and horses, and the tramplings of their feet in this battle.'

———

ELIOT.

AFTER a pathetic account of Eliot's long imprisonment in the Tower, of his continued illness, and the disregard of the petitions from himself and his friends that he should be released, to try the effect of the only remedies, air and exercise, Forster cites Eliot's answer to the Keeper of the Tower, who urged him to humble himself to the King, and crave pardon,—' I thank you, sir, for your friendly advice : but my spirits are growen feeble and faint, which when it shall please God to restore unto their former vigour, I shall take it further into my consideration.'

And in these words Forster concludes his faithful life of the patriot :—

' It was not God's pleasure that he should ever be restored. He was now reclaiming to Himself that good and faithful servant, whose work on the earth was done. The same news-writer describes in another letter his meeting with Sir John Eliot's Attorney in Saint Paul's churchyard on the night of the 12th of November, and hearing from him that he had been that morning with Sir John in the Tower, and found him so far spent with consumption that he was not likely to live a week longer. He lived fifteen days. It was not until the 27th November, 1632, that the welcome tidings could be carried to Whitehall that Sir John Eliot was dead. He had passed away that morning in his forty-third year.

' But revenges there are which death cannot satisfy, and natures that will not drop their hatreds at the grave. The son desired to carry his father's remains to Port Eliot, there to lie with those of his ancestors ; and the King was addressed once more. The youth drew up a humble petition that his Majesty would be pleased to permit the body of his father to be carried into Cornwall to be buried there. Whereto was answered at the foot of the petition, "*Lette Sir John Eliot's body be buried in the Churche of the parish where he dyed.*" And so he was buried in the Tower.

' No stone marks the spot where he lies, but as long as Freedom continues in England he will not be without a monument.'

TRELAWNY.

SOME who are familiar with this good name, and who join in singing the fine ballad Mr. Hawker composed as he told us under a staghorned oak in Sir Beville's walk in Stowe Wood, may not be so well acquainted with the historic facts which have made Trelawny famous. They are set out with fidelity in Hume's History of England, from which the subjoined extracts are taken.

The King, James II., having without the sanction of Parliament promulgated a second declaration of indulgence which had for its real object the protection and encouragement of the Roman Catholic faith, and having required that the indulgence should be read by the clergy in all churches, six Bishops, including Trelawny, then Bishop of Bristol, met the Primate, and agreed to a loyal petition of remonstrance. On this the King decided to prosecute the Bishops for sedition, and ordered them, as

c 2

they declined to give bail, to be committed to the Tower.
'The people,' says the historian, 'were already aware of
the danger to which the prelates were exposed ; and were
raised to the highest pitch of anxiety and attention with
regard to the issue of this extraordinary affair ; but when
they beheld the fathers of the church brought from court
under the custody of a guard ; when they saw them em-
bark in vessels on the river, and conveyed towards the
Tower, all their affection for liberty, all their zeal for
religion blazed up at once ; and they flew to behold this
afflicting spectacle. The whole shore was covered
with crowds of prostrate spectators, who at once implored
the blessing of those holy pastors, and addressed their
petitions towards Heaven for protection during the extreme danger to which their country and their religion
stood exposed. Even the soldiers, siezed with the
contagion of the same spirit, flung themselves on their
knees before the distressed prelates, and craved the bene-
diction of those criminals whom they were appointed to
guard.'

'Their passage, when conducted to their trial, was, if
possible, attended by greater crowds of anxious spectators :
all men saw the dangerous crisis to which affairs were
reduced, and were sensible that the king could not have
put the issue on a cause more unfavourable for himself
than that in which he had so imprudently engaged.
Twenty-nine temporal peers (for the other prelates kept
aloof) attended the prisoners to Westminster Hall : and
such crowds of gentry followed the procession, that
scarcely was any room left for the populace to enter.'

After summarising the pleading of the counsel for the
Bishops, the historian thus concludes his account of this
memorable trial : —'These arguments were convincing in

themselves, and were heard with a favourable disposition by the audience : even some of the Judges, though their seats were held during pleasure, declared themselves in favour of the prisoners ; the Jury, however, (from what cause is unknown) took several hours to deliberate, and kept, during so long a time, the people in the most anxious expectation ; but when the wished-for verdict, ' Not Guilty,' was at last pronounced (June 30, 1688), the intelligence was echoed through the hall, was conveyed to the crowds without, was carried into the City, and was propagated with infinite joy throughout the kingdom.'

There is a portrait of the Prelate to be seen among other portraits of the Trelawny family at their seat, Trelawne. One of the late members for the Eastern Division of Cornwall, Sir John Trelawny, is a descendant of the Bishop.

VIVIAN.

THIS distinguished Cornishman entered the army in July, 1793, and in 1794 and 1795 he served as Captain in the 28th Regiment in Flanders and Holland under the Duke of York. In 1799, as Captain in the 7th Hussars, he joined the Expedition to the Helder. In 1808 he, as Colonel of the 7th Hussars, commanded that regiment in the expedition under Sir John Moore. In 1813 he again served in the Peninsula with the Army under Wellington, as Colonel on the Staff in command of a brigade of Cavalry. In 1815, as Major-General, he commanded a brigade of Cavalry at Waterloo. How he led that brigade in the final charge Alison has described in the History of

Europe (vol xii. pp. 253 to 259). Gourgaud, the Emperor's
aide-de-camp, ascribes the loss of the battle mainly to
this happy charge of Vivian's brigade on the flank of the
Old Guard, after the repulse of the Middle. 'The sun,'
he says, ' was set, nothing was despaired of when the
brigades of the enemy's cavalry, who had not yet charged,
penetrated between La Haye Sainte and the corps of
General Reille. They might have been stopped by the
four squares of the Guard, but seeing the great disorder
which prevailed towards the right, they turned. These
three thousand cavalry prevented all rallying.' In 1831
he was named to the command of the Army in Ireland,
where he was seven times one of the Lords Justices.
From Ireland he was brought to fill the office of Master
General of the Ordnance. He sat in all the Parliaments
(with the exception of one) from 1820 to 1841, when he
was raised to the Peerage, having been twice elected for
Truro, twice for Windsor, and once for East Cornwall.
He was Lieutenant-General in the Army, Grand Cross of
the Bath, and Knight of several Foreign Orders. He was
a Privy Councillor both in England and Ireland. His
death occurred at Baden on the 20th August, 1842, and he
was, by his own direction, buried in the cemetery of St.
Mary's, Truro (his native town), by the side of his
parents. On the monument which was erected in that
church, and which will now be placed in the cathedral, his
features are faithfully sculptured; and there is a picture
of him by Shee at Glynn, the family seat; but no artist
could do justice to that noble presence. The writer has
an engraving by Meyer of this picture, which stood for
many years by the bedside of the Chelsea pensioner who
had attended the late lord in his campaigns. The old
soldier had frequently been offered a considerable sum for

the engraving, but he would not part with it; and just before his death he requested that it should be sent to the late lord's second son, the late Capt. J. C. W. Vivian, by whom it was given to the writer.

Lord Vivian's sons inherited his military bias, as well as his ambition to serve the country in Parliament and otherwise. The present Lord was M.P. for Bodmin for some years, and in 1856 he was appointed Lord Lieutenant of Cornwall, and continued till 1877 to perform the duties of that office with equal honour to himself and advantage to the county. Capt. Vivian was first returned for Penryn and Falmouth; he afterwards sat for Bodmin; and for many years, and until his appointment as Permanent Secretary for War, represented Truro.

FATHER AND SON.

These lines were first printed for private circulation, as a memorial of Richard Foster, Esq., of Castle, Lostwithiel, and of his son, Lieut. Ed. Foster, R.N. The former, as a Magistrate for the county, and of which he had also been Sheriff, had earned the public approbation by a most assiduous and considerate discharge of his duties. He died on the 27th January, 1869, from the effects of a small bone which he had swallowed, while in the vigour of his health and faculties; and his son, who had for some time been invalided from H.M.S. Galatea, in which he had sailed with H.R.H. the Duke of Edinburgh, died at the father's house on the 30th of the same month. The circumstances attending these bereavements elicited a general expression of sympathy.

THE CAPTAIN.

The ironclad turret-ship Captain was lost off Cape Finisterre on the 7th September, 1870. Sir Alexander Milne, who was on board the Lord Warden, thus reported :—'The *Captain* was close to this ship at two in morning. Then there was a sudden south-west gale, with heavy squalls ; at day-break the *Captain* was missing.'

When the survivors of the crew of the ill fated ship were all honourably acquitted by the Court Martial, the conduct of several elicited public admiration. The gunner, Mr. May, and the seaman, Heard, both of whom stood by Capt. Burgoyne to the last while on the keel of the pinnace, received special approval. But, in Cornwall, the manner in which Charles Tregenna of Bude steered the rudderless launch with his oar for twelve hours naturally elicited warm plaudits. Speaking of him, May said he steered the boat splendidly ; and while he reported that the conduct of all was excellent, he repeated at the close of his evidence that the only distinction he could make between them was in Tregenna's case.

THE PLAINT OF MORWENSTOW.

Robert Stephen Hawker, to whom these stanzas refer, was born at Plymouth, Dec. 3rd, 1804. He was son of Jacob Stephen Hawker, Vicar of Stratton, and grandson of Dr. Hawker, incumbent of Charles Church, Plymouth. He graduated at Oxford in 1828, having obtained the Newdegate in 1827, for his poem 'Pompeii.' In 1834 he was appointed Vicar of Morwenstow, and so continued till his death at Plymouth on the 15th August, 1875. On the 9th of that month he was struck down with paralysis, and was in a semi-conscious state for some days before his death. But on Saturday, 14th August, he was visited by the Roman Catholic Canon Mansfield, and the Sacraments of that church were then administered to him; and on the 18th of August his body was taken from the Roman Catholic Cathedral at Plymouth to the cemetery of that town.

Those who desire information respecting the incidents of the last few days of Mr. Hawker's life will find interesting details in the biographies by Mr. Baring Gould and Dr. Lee. To infer from his reception into the Roman Catholic Church on his death-bed that he had deliberately practised deception and hypocrisy during any portion of his long life, is to do cruel wrong to his character and memory; and, notwithstanding the controversy that has arisen, there are few who really knew him who will not continue to regard him as a true man, a genuine poet, and a sincere christian.

On the Tuesday before his death he was grieving that he could not return to his dear old Church; and it cannot be doubted that he would have yet more deeply grieved in his last hours, if he had been told that his remains were not to be buried in his own Churchyard in the grave where a place had been reserved by his own orders for his sepulture.

When the Poet of Cornwall last looked on the Atlantic from the cliff of Morwenstow, he little thought that one of the most admired and best loved of the American poets, the author of Evangeline, was then engaged at Cambridge, Massachusetts, in making extracts from his poems. Another poet, who had not published any of the Idylls of the King when he was the Vicar's guest, sent cordial remembrances to him not long before the Vicar himself left his hospitable home by the 'Severn Sea' to return to it no more.

Stanza 4.

Relying on the authority of Mr. Halliwell Phillips, I have given the words in the third line as they appear in the original text of Hamlet, act i, scene 5. The meaning of the words is said to be as follows :—'unhousell'd,' without having received the sacrament; 'disappointed,' unprepared; 'unaneled,' without extreme unction.

LANHYDROCK.

To this elegy, as printed separately in 1882, a full biographical note is appended. Here it may suffice to state that the late Lord Robartes was born in 1808, and on the death of his mother, the Hon. Anna Maria Agar, he became owner of Lanhydrock and other extensive properties as the legal heir and representative of the Robartes family, of whom four were Earls of Radnor. On the death of the fourth Earl without male issue the title became extinct. The late lord by royal license added the name of Robartes to that of Agar. He was educated at Harrow and Oxford. From 1847 to 1868 he represented East Cornwall in Parliament, as one of its members, and in 1869 he was created a peer, with the title of Baron Robartes of Lanhydrock and Truro. His wife, the exemplary lady mentioned in the elegy, was a daughter of the Hon. Pole Carew of Antony. The present lord, their only child, was educated at Oxford, and when he succeeded to the title he was one of the members for East Cornwall.

Truro was the birth-place of the remoter ancestors of the family, and in the church of Saint Mary in that town, now incorporated with the Cathedral, there is a tablet in memory of one of those ancestors, John Robartes, who died in 1615, on which the following words are inscribed in the style and spelling of the age:—" He was in all his 'life-time a true lover of vertue, in word and deed plain, upright, truthful and constant, and most just in per- 'forming the same; and evermore in his actions reputed grave, honest, and very discreet.' Towards the close of the sermon preached in the Cathedral by the Rev. Chancellor Whitaker on the day of the late lord's funeral, the preacher said—' Thank God we can believe these words to be true of him whom Cornwall mourns to-day. God grant us that when we die our memory, like his, may be a source of strength and blessing to our children after us !'

BODMIN
PRINTED BY LIDDELL AND SON

JULY 1884.

GENERAL LISTS OF WORKS

PUBLISHED BY

MESSRS. LONGMANS, GREEN, & CO.

PATERNOSTER ROW, LONDON.

HISTORY, POLITICS, HISTORICAL MEMOIRS, &c.

Arnold's Lectures on Modern History. 8vo. 7s. 6d.
Bagehot's Literary Studies, edited by Hutton. 2 vols. 8vo. 28s.
Beaconsfield's (Lord) Speeches, by Kebbel. 2 vols. 8vo. 32s.
Bramston & Leroy's Historic Winchester. Crown 8vo. 6s.
Buckle's History of Civilisation. 3 vols. crown 8vo. 24s.
Chesney's Waterloo Lectures. 8vo. 10s. 6d.
Cox's (Sir G. W.) General History of Greece. Crown 8vo. Maps, 7s. 6d.
Doyle's English in America. 8vo. 18s.

Epochs of Ancient History :—
        Beesly's Gracchi, Marius, and Sulla, 2s. 6d.
        Capes's Age of the Antonines, 2s. 6d.
        — Early Roman Empire, 2s. 6d.
        Cox's Athenian Empire, 2s. 6d.
        — Greeks and Persians, 2s. 6d.
        Curteis's Rise of the Macedonian Empire, 2s. 6d.
        Ihne's Rome to its Capture by the Gauls, 2s. 6d.
        Merivale's Roman Triumvirates, 2s. 6d.
        Sankey's Spartan and Theban Supremacies, 2s. 6d.
        Smith's Rome and Carthage, the Punic Wars, 2s. 6d.

Epochs of English History, complete in One Volume. Fcp. 8vo. 5s.
        Browning's Modern England, 1820-1874, 9d.
        Creighton's Shilling History of England (Introductory Volume).
        Fcp. 8vo. 1s.
        Creighton's (Mrs.) England a Continental Power, 1066-1216, 9d.
        Creighton's (Rev. M.) Tudors and the Reformation, 1485-1603, 9d.
        Gardiner's (Mrs.) Struggle against Absolute Monarchy, 1603-
        1688, 9d.
        Rowley's Rise of the People, 1215-1485, 9d.
        Rowley's Settlement of the Constitution, 1689-1784, 9d.
        Tancock's England during the American & European Wars,
        1765-1820, 9d.
        York-Powell's Early England to the Conquest, 1s.

Epochs of Modern History :—
        Church's Beginning of the Middle Ages, 2s. 6d.
        Cox's Crusades, 2s. 6d.
        Creighton's Age of Elizabeth, 2s. 6d. [Continued on page 2.

London, LONGMANS & CO.

Epochs of Modern History—*continued.*

Gairdner's Houses of Lancaster and York, 2*s.* 6*d.*
Gardiner's Puritan Revolution, 2*s.* 6*d.*
  — Thirty Years' War, 2*s.* 6*d.*
  — (Mrs.) French Revolution, 1789–1795, 2*s.* 6*d.*
Hale's Fall of the Stuarts, 2*s.* 6*d.*
Johnson's Normans in Europe, 2*s.* 6*d.*
Longman's Frederick the Great and the Seven Years' War, 2*s.* 6*d.*
Ludlow's War of American Independence, 2*s.* 6*d.*
M'Carthy's Epoch of Reform, 1830–1850, 2*s.* 6*d.*
Morris's Age of Queen Anne, 2*s.* 6*d.*
Seebohm's Protestant Revolution, 2*s.* 6*d.*
Stubbs's Early Plantagenets, 2*s.* 6*d.*
Warburton's Edward III., 2*s.* 6*d.*

Froude's English in Ireland in the 18th Century. 3 vols. crown 8vo. 18*s.*
  — History of England. Popular Edition. 12 vols. crown 8vo. 3*s.* 6*d.* each.
Gardiner's History of England from the Accession of James I. to the Outbreak of the Civil War. 10 vols. crown 8vo. 60*s.*
  — Outline of English History, B.C. 55–A.D. 1880. Fcp. 8vo. 2*s.* 6*d.*
Grant's (Sir Alex.) The Story of the University of Edinburgh. 2 vols. 8vo. 36*s.*
Greville's Journal of the Reigns of George IV. & William IV. 3 vols. 8vo. 36*s.*
Hickson's Ireland in the Seventeenth Century. 2 vols. 8vo. 28*s.*
Lecky's History of England. Vols. I. & II. 1700–1760. 8vo. 36*s.* Vols. III. & IV. 1760–1784. 8vo. 36*s.*
  — History of European Morals. 2 vols. crown 8vo. 16*s.*
  — — — Rationalism in Europe. 2 vols. crown 8vo. 16*s.*
Lewes's History of Philosophy. 2 vols. 8vo. 32*s.*
Longman's Lectures on the History of England. 8vo. 15*s.*
  — Life and Times of Edward III. 2 vols. 8vo. 28*s.*
Macaulay's Complete Works. Library Edition. 8 vols. 8vo. £5. 5*s.*
  — — — Cabinet Edition. 16 vols. crown 8vo. £4. 16*s.*
  — History of England :—

Student's Edition. 2 vols. cr. 8vo. 12*s.* | Cabinet Edition. 8 vols. post 8vo. 48*s.*
People's Edition. 4 vols. cr. 8vo. 16*s.* | Library Edition. 5 vols. 8vo. £4.

Macaulay's Critical and Historical Essays. Cheap Edition. Crown 8vo. 2*s.* 6*d.*
Student's Edition. 1 vol. cr. 8vo. 6*s.* | Cabinet Edition. 4 vols. post 8vo. 24*s.*
People's Edition. 2 vols. cr. 8vo. 8*s.* | Library Edition. 3 vols. 8vo. 36*s.*

Maxwell's (Sir W. S.) Don John of Austria. Library Edition, with numerous Illustrations. 2 vols. Royal 8vo. 42*s.*
May's Constitutional History of England, 1760–1870. 3 vols. crown 8vo. 18*s.*
  — Democracy in Europe. 2 vols. 8vo. 32*s.*
Merivale's Fall of the Roman Republic. 12mo. 7*s.* 6*d.*
  — General History of Rome, B.C. 753—A.D. 476. Crown 8vo. 7*s.* 6*d.*
  — History of the Romans under the Empire. 8 vols. post 8vo. 48*s.*
Rawlinson's Seventh Great Oriental Monarchy—The Sassanians. 8vo. 28*s.*
Seebohm's Oxford Reformers—Colet, Erasmus, & More. 8vo. 14*s.*
Short's History of the Church of England. Crown 8vo. 7*s.* 6*d.*
Smith's Carthage and the Carthaginians. Crown 8vo. 10*s.* 6*d.*
Taylor's Manual of the History of India. Crown 8vo. 7*s.* 6*d.*
Trevelyan's Early History of Charles James Fox. Crown 8vo. 6*s.*
Walpole's History of England, 1815–1841. 3 vols. 8vo. £2. 14*s.*

London, LONGMANS & CO.

BIOGRAPHICAL WORKS.

Bagehot's Biographical Studies. 1 vol. 8vo. 12*s*.

Bain's Biography of James Mill. Crown 8vo. Portrait, 5*s*.
— Criticism and Recollections of J. S. Mill. Crown 8vo. 2*s*. 6*d*.

Carlyle's Reminiscences, edited by J. A. Froude. 2 vols. crown 8vo. 18*s*.
— (Mrs.) Letters and Memorials. 3 vols. 8vo. 36*s*.

Oates's Dictionary of General Biography. Medium 8vo. 28*s*.

Froude's Luther, a short Biography. Crown 8vo. 1*s*.
— Thomas Carlyle. Vols. 1 & 2, 1795–1835. 8vo. with Portraits and Plates, 32*s*.

Gleig's Life of the Duke of Wellington. Crown 8vo. 6*s*.

Halliwell-Phillipps's Outlines of Shakespeare's Life. 8vo. 7*s*. 6*d*.

Lecky's Leaders of Public Opinion in Ireland. Crown 8vo. 7*s*. 6*d*.

Life (The) and Letters of Lord Macaulay. By his Nephew, G. Otto Trevelyan, M.P. Popular Edition, 1 vol. crown 8vo. 6*s*. Cabinet Edition, 2 vols. post 8vo. 12*s*. Library Edition, 2 vols. 8vo. 36*s*.

Marshman's Memoirs of Havelock. Crown 8vo. 3*s*. 6*d*.

Mendelssohn's Letters. Translated by Lady Wallace. 2 vols. cr. 8vo. 5*s*. each.

Mill's (John Stuart) Autobiography. 8vo. 7*s*. 6*d*.

Mozley's Reminiscences of Oriel College. 2 vols. crown 8vo. 18*s*.

Newman's Apologia pro Vitâ Suâ. Crown 8vo. 6*s*.

Skobeleff & the Slavonic Cause. By O. K. 8vo. Portrait, 14*s*.

Southey's Correspondence with Caroline Bowles. 8vo. 14*s*.

Spedding's Letters and Life of Francis Bacon. 7 vols. 8vo. £4. 4*s*.

Stephen's Essays in Ecclesiastical Biography. Crown 8vo. 7*s*. 6*d*.

MENTAL AND POLITICAL PHILOSOPHY.

Amos's View of the Science of Jurisprudence. 8vo. 18*s*.
— Fifty Years of the English Constitution, 1830–1880. Crown 8vo. 10*s*. 6*d*.
— Primer of the English Constitution. Crown 8vo. 6*s*.

Bacon's Essays, with Annotations by Whately. 8vo. 10*s*. 6*d*.
— Promus, edited by Mrs. H. Pott. 8vo. 16*s*.
— Works, edited by Spedding. 7 vols. 8vo. 73*s*. 6*d*.

Bagehot's Economic Studies, edited by Hutton. 8vo. 10*s*. 6*d*.

Bain's Logic, Deductive and Inductive. Crown 8vo. 10*s*. 6*d*.
PART I. Deduction, 4*s*. | PART II. Induction, 6*s*. 6*d*.

Bolland & Lang's Aristotle's Politics. Crown 8vo. 7*s*. 6*d*.

Grant's Ethics of Aristotle; Greek Text, English Notes. 2 vols. 8vo. 32*s*.

Hodgson's Philosophy of Reflection. 2 vols. 8vo. 21*s*.

Kalisch's Path and Goal. 8vo. 12*s*. 6*d*.

Leslie's Essays in Political and Moral Philosophy. 8vo. 10*s*. 6*d*.

Lewis on Authority in Matters of Opinion. 8vo. 14*s*.

Macaulay's Speeches corrected by Himself. Crown 8vo. 3*s*. 6*d*.

Macleod's Economical Philosophy. Vol. I. 8vo. 15*s*. Vol. II. Part I. 12*s*.

Mill's (James) Analysis of the Phenomena of the Human Mind. 2 vols. 8vo. 28*s*.

Mill (John Stuart) on Representative Government. Crown 8vo. 2*s*.
— — on Liberty. Crown 8vo. 1*s*. 4*d*.

Mill's (John Stuart) Dissertations and Discussions. 4 vols. 8vo. 46*s*. 6*d*.

London, LONGMANS & CO.

Mill's (John Stuart) Essays on Unsettled Questions of Political Economy. 8vo.
6*s*. 6*d*.
—   —   Examination of Hamilton's Philosophy. 8vo. 16*s*.
—   —   Logic, Ratiocinative and Inductive. 2 vols. 8vo. 25*s*.
—   —   Principles of Political Economy. 2 vols. 8vo. 30*s*. 1 vol.
crown 8vo. 5*s*.
—   —   Subjection of Women. Crown 8vo. 6*s*.
—   ' —   Utilitarianism. 8vo. 5*s*.
Miller's (Mrs. Fenwick) Readings in Social Economy. Crown 8vo. 5*s*.
Sandars's Institutes of Justinian, with English Notes. 8vo. 18*s*.
Seebohm's English Village Community. 8vo. 16*s*.
Sully's Outlines of Psychology. 8vo. 12*s*. 6*d*.
Swinburne's Picture Logic. Post 8vo. 5*s*.
Thomson's Outline of Necessary Laws of Thought. Crown 8vo. 6*s*.
Tocqueville's Democracy in America, translated by Reeve. 2 vols. crown 8vo. 16*s*.
Twiss's Law of Nations in Time of War. 8vo. 21*s*.
Whately's Elements of Logic. 8vo. 10*s*. 6*d*. Crown 8vo. 4*s*. 6*d*.
—   —   — Rhetoric. 8vo. 10*s*. 6*d*. Crown 8vo. 4*s*. 6*d*.
—   English Synonymes. Fcp. 8vo. 3*s*.
Williams's Nicomachean Ethics of Aristotle translated. Crown 8vo. 7*s*. 6*d*.
Zeller's History of Eclecticism in Greek Philosophy. Crown 8vo. 10*s*. 6*d*.
—   Plato and the Older Academy. Crown 8vo. 18*s*.
—   Pre-Socratic Schools. 2 vols. crown 8vo. 30*s*.
—   Socrates and the Socratic Schools. Crown 8vo. 10*s*. 6*d*.
—   Stoics, Epicureans, and Sceptics. Crown 8vo. 15*s*.

MISCELLANEOUS AND CRITICAL WORKS.

Arnold's (Dr. Thomas) Miscellaneous Works. 8vo. 7*s*. 6*d*.
—   (T.) Manual of English Literature. Crown 8vo. 7*s*. 6*d*.
Bain's Emotions and the Will. 8vo. 15*s*.
—   Mental and Moral Science. Crown 8vo. 10*s*. 6*d*.
—   Senses and the Intellect. 8vo. 15*s*.
—   Practical Essays. Crown 8vo. 4*s*. 6*d*.
Beaconsfield (Lord), The Wit and Wisdom of. Crown 8vo. 3*s*. 6*d*.
—   (The) Birthday Book. 18mo. 2*s*. 6*d*. cloth ; 4*s*. 6*d*. bound.
Becker's *Charicles* and *Gallus*, by Metcalfe. Post 8vo. 7*s*. 6*d*. each.
Blackley's German and English Dictionary. Post 8vo. 7*s*. 6*d*.
Contanseau's Practical French & English Dictionary. Post 8vo. 3*s*. 6*d*.
—   Pocket French and English Dictionary. Square 18mo. 1*s*. 6*d*.
Farrar's Language and Languages. Crown 8vo. 6*s*.
French's Nineteen Centuries of Drink in England. Crown 8vo. 10*s*. 6*d*.
Froude's Short Studies on Great Subjects. 4 vols. crown 8vo. 24*s*.
Grant's (Sir A.) Story of the University of Edinburgh. 2 vols. 8vo. 36*s*.
Hobart's Medical Language of St. Luke. 8vo. 16*s*.
Hume's Essays, edited by Green & Grose. 2 vols. 8vo. 28*s*.
—   Treatise on Human Nature, edited by Green & Grose. 2 vols. 8vo. 28*s*.
Latham's Handbook of the English Language. Crown 8vo. 6*s*.
Liddell & Scott's Greek-English Lexicon. 4to. 36*s*.
—   Abridged Greek-English Lexicon. Square 12mo. 7*s*. 6*d*.
Longman's Pocket German and English Dictionary. 18mo. 5*s*.
Macaulay's Miscellaneous Writings. 2 vols. 8vo. 21*s*. 1 vol. crown 8vo. 4*s*. 6*d*.
—   Miscellaneous Writings and Speeches. Crown 8vo. 6*s*.
—   Miscellaneous Writings, Speeches, Lays of Ancient Rome, &c.
Cabinet Edition. 4 vols. crown 8vo. 24*s*.

London, LONGMANS & CO.

Mahaffy's Classical Greek Literature. Crown 8vo. Vol. I. the Poets, 7*s.* 6*d.*
Vol. II. the Prose Writers, 7*s.* 6*d.*
Millard's Grammar of Elocution. Fcp. 8vo. 3*s.* 6*d.*
Milner's Country Pleasures. Crown 8vo. 6*s.*
Müller's (Max) Lectures on the Science of Language. 2 vols. crown 8vo. 16*s.*
— — Lectures on India. 8vo. 12*s.* 6*d.*
Rich's Dictionary of Roman and Greek Antiquities. Crown 8vo. 7*s.* 6*d.*
Rogers's Eclipse of Faith. Fcp. 8vo. 5*s.*
— Defence of the Eclipse of Faith Fcp. 8vo. 3*s.* 6*d.*
Roget's Thesaurus of English Words and Phrases. Crown 8vo. 10*s.* 6*d.*
Selections from the Writings of Lord Macaulay. Crown 8vo. 6*s.*
Simcox's Latin Literature. 2 vols. 8vo. 32*s.*
Tyndall's Faraday as a Discoverer. Crown 8vo. 3*s.* 6*d.*
— . Floating Matter of the Air. Crown 8vo. 7*s.* 6*d.*
— Fragments of Science. 2 vols. post 8vo. 16*s.*
— Heat a Mode of Motion. Crown 8vo. 12*s.*
— Lectures on Light delivered in America. Crown 8vo. 7*s.* 6*d.*
— Lessons in Electricity. Crown 8vo. 2*s.* 6*d.*
— Notes on Electrical Phenomena. Crown 8vo. 1*s.* sewed, 1*s.* 6*d.* cloth.
— Notes of Lectures on Light. Crown 8vo. 1*s.* sewed, 1*s.* 6*d.* cloth.
— Sound, with Frontispiece & 203 Woodcuts. Crown 8vo. 10*s.* 6*d.*
Von Cotta on Rocks, by Lawrence. Post 8vo. 14*s.*
White & Riddle's Large Latin-English Dictionary. 4to. 21*s.*
White's Concise Latin-English Dictionary. Royal 8vo. 12*s.*
— Junior Student's Lat.-Eng. and Eng.-Lat. Dictionary. Sq. 12mo. 5*s.*
Separately { The English-Latin Dictionary, 3*s.*
{ The Latin-English Dictionary, 3*s.*
Wit and **Wisdom** of the Rev. Sydney Smith, Crown 8vo. 3*s.* 6*d.*
Witt's Myths of Hellas, translated by F. M. Younghusband. Crown 8vo. 3*s.* 6*d.*
— The Trojan War. Fcp. 8vo. 2*s.*
Wood's Bible Animals. With 112 Vignettes. 8vo. 10*s.* 6*d.*
— Common British Insects. Crown 8vo. 3*s.* 6*d.*
— Homes Without Hands. 8vo. 10*s.* 6*d.* Insects Abroad. 8vo. 10*s.* 6*d.*
— Insects at Home. With 700 Illustrations. 8vo. 10*s.* 6*d.*
— Out of Doors. Crown 8vo. 5*s.*
— Petland Revisited. Crown 8vo. 7*s.* 6*d.*
— Strange Dwellings. Crown 8vo. 5*s.* Popular Edition, 4to. 6*d.*
Yonge's English-Greek Lexicon. Square 12mo. 8*s.* 6*d.* 4to. 21*s.*
The Essays and Contributions of A. K. H. B. Crown 8vo.
Autumn Holidays of a Country Parson. 3*s.* 6*d.*
Changed Aspects of Unchanged Truths. 3*s.* 6*d.*
Common-place Philosopher in Town and Country. 3*s.* 6*d.*
Counsel and Comfort spoken from a City Pulpit. 3*s.* 6*d.*
Critical Essays of a Country Parson. 3*s.* 6*d.*
Graver Thoughts of a Country Parson. Three Series, 3*s.* 6*d.* each.
Landscapes, Churches, and Moralities. 3*s.* 6*d.*
Leisure Hours in Town. 3*s.* 6*d.* Lessons of Middle Age. 3*s.* 6*d.*
Our Little Life. Essays Consolatory and Domestic. 3*s.* 6*d.*
Present-day Thoughts. 3*s.* 6*d.*
Recreations of a Country Parson. Three Series, 3*s.* 6*d.* each.
Seaside Musings on Sundays and Week-Days. 3*s.* 6*d.*
Sunday Afternoons in the Parish Church of a University City. 3*s.* 6*d.*

London, LONGMANS & CO.

ASTRONOMY, METEOROLOGY, GEOGRAPHY, &c.

Freeman's Historical Geography of Europe. 2 vols. 8vo. 31s. 6d.
Herschel's Outlines of Astronomy. Square crown 8vo. 12s.
Keith Johnston's Dictionary of Geography, or General Gazetteer. 8vo. 42s.
Merrifield's Treatise on Navigation. Crown 8vo. 5s.
Nelson's Work on the Moon. Medium 8vo. 31s. 6d.
Proctor's Essays on Astronomy. 8vo. 12s.   Proctor's Moon. Crown 8vo. 10s. 6d.
—   Larger Star Atlas. Folio, 15s. or Maps only, 12s. 6d.
—   Myths and Marvels of Astronomy. Crown 8vo. 6s.
—   New Star Atlas. Crown 8vo. 5s.   Orbs Around Us. Crown 8vo. 7s. 6d.
—   Other Worlds than Ours. Crown 8vo. 10s. 6d.
—   Sun. Crown 8vo. 14s.   Universe of Stars. 8vo. 10s. 6d.
—   Transits of Venus, 8vo. 8s. 6d.   Studies of Venus-Transits, 8vo. 5s.
Smith's Air and Rain. 8vo. 24s.
The Public Schools Atlas of Ancient Geography. Imperial 8vo. 7s. 6d.
—   —   —   Modern Geography. Imperial 8vo. 5s.
Webb's Celestial Objects for Common Telescopes. Crown 8vo. 9s.

NATURAL HISTORY & POPULAR SCIENCE. :

Allen's Flowers and their Pedigrees. Crown 8vo. Woodcuts, 7s. 6d.
Arnott's Elements of Physics or Natural Philosophy. Crown 8vo. 12s. 6d.
Brande's Dictionary of Science, Literature, and Art. 3 vols. medium 8vo. 63s.
Decaisne and Le Maout's General System of Botany. Imperial 8vo. 31s. 6d.
Dixon's Rural Bird Life. Crown 8vo. Illustrations, 5s.
Edmonds's Elementary Botany. Fcp. 8vo. 2s.
Evans's Bronze Implements of Great Britain. 8vo. 25s.
Ganot's Elementary Treatise on Physics, by Atkinson. Large crown 8vo. 15s.
—   Natural Philosophy, by Atkinson. Crown 8vo. 7s. 6d.
Goodeve's Elements of Mechanism. Crown 8vo. 6s.
—   Principles of Mechanics. Crown 8vo. 6s.
Grove's Correlation of Physical Forces. 8vo. 15s.
Hartwig's Aerial World. 8vo. 10s. 6d.   Polar World. 8vo. 10s. 6d.
—   Sea and its Living Wonders. 8vo. 10s. 6d.
—   Subterranean World. 8vo. 10s. 6d.   Tropical World. 8vo. 10s. 6d.
Haughton's Six Lectures on Physical Geography. 8vo. 15s.
Heer's Primæval World of Switzerland. 2 vols. 8vo. 12s.
Helmholtz's Lectures on Scientific Subjects. 2 vols. cr. 8vo. 7s. 6d. each.
Hullah's Lectures on the History of Modern Music. 8vo. 8s. 6d.
—   Transition Period of Musical History. 8vo. 10s. 6d.
Jones's The Health of the Senses. Crown 8vo. 3s. 6d.
Keller's Lake Dwellings of Switzerland, by Lee. 2 vols. royal 8vo. 42s.
Lloyd's Treatise on Magnetism. 8vo. 10s. 6d.
London's Encyclopædia of Plants. 8vo. 42s.
Lubbock on the Origin of Civilisation & Primitive Condition of Man. 8vo. 18s.
Macalister's Zoology and Morphology of Vertebrate Animals. 8vo. 10s. 6d.
Nicols' Puzzle of Life. Crown 8vo. 3s. 6d.
Owen's Comparative Anatomy and Physiology of the Vertebrate Animals. 3 vols.
8vo. 73s. 6d.
—   Experimental Physiology. Crown 8vo. 5s.
Proctor's Light Science for Leisure Hours. 3 Series, crown 8vo. 7s. 6d. each.
Rivers's Orchard House. Sixteenth Edition. Crown 8vo. 5s.
—   Rose Amateur's Guide. Fcp. 8vo. 4s. 6d.
Stanley's Familiar History of British Birds. Crown 8vo. 6s.
Swinton's Electric Lighting : Its Principles and Practice. Crown 8vo. 5s.

London, LONGMANS & CO.

THE 'KNOWLEDGE' LIBRARY,

Edited by RICHARD A. PROCTOR.

The Borderland of Science. By R. A. Proctor. Crown 8vo. 6s.
Science Byways. By R. A. Proctor. Crown 8vo. 6s.
The Poetry of Astronomy. By R. A. Proctor. Crown 8vo. 6s.
Nature Studies. Reprinted from *Knowledge*. By Grant Allen, Andrew Wilson, &c. Crown 8vo. 6s.
Leisure Readings. Reprinted from *Knowledge*. By Edward Clodd, Andrew Wilson, &c. Crown 8vo. 6s.
The Stars in their Seasons. By R. A. Proctor. Imperial 8vo. 5s.

CHEMISTRY AND PHYSIOLOGY.

Buckton's Health in the House, Lectures on Elementary Physiology. Cr. 8vo. 2s.
Jago's Inorganic Chemistry, Theoretical and Practical. Fcp. 8vo. 2s.
Kolbe's Short Text-Book of Inorganic Chemistry. Crown 8vo. 7s. 6d.
Miller's Elements of Chemistry, Theoretical and Practical. 3 vols. 8vo. Part I. Chemical Physics, 16s. Part II. Inorganic Chemistry, 24s. Part III. Organic Chemistry, price 31s. 6d.
Reynolds's Experimental Chemistry. Fcp. 8vo. Pt. I. 1s. 6d. Pt. II. 2s. 6d. Pt. III. 3s. 6d.
Tilden's Practical Chemistry. Fcp. 8vo. 1s. 6d.
Watts's Dictionary of Chemistry. 9 vols. medium 8vo. £15. 2s. 6d.

THE FINE ARTS AND ILLUSTRATED EDITIONS.

Dresser's Arts and Art Manufactures of Japan. Square crown 8vo. 31s. 6d.
Eastlake's (Lady) Five Great Painters. 2 vols. crown 8vo. 16s.
— Notes on the Brera Gallery, Milan. Crown 8vo. 5s.
— Notes on the Louvre Gallery, Paris. Crown 8vo. 7s. 6d.
Hulme's Art-Instruction in England. Fcp. 8vo. 3s. 6d.
Jameson's Sacred and Legendary Art. 6 vols. square crown 8vo.
Legends of the Madonna. 1 vol. 21s.
— — — Monastic Orders. 1 vol. 21s.
— — — Saints and Martyrs. 2 vols. 31s. 6d.
— — — Saviour. Completed by Lady Eastlake. 2 vols. 42s.
Macaulay's Lays of Ancient Rome, illustrated by Scharf. Fcp. 4to. 10s. 6d.
The same, with *Ivry* and the *Armada*, illustrated by Weguelin. Crown 8vo. 3s. 6d.
Macfarren's Lectures on Harmony. 8vo. 12s.
Moore's Irish Melodies. With 161 Plates by D. Maclise, R.A. Super-royal 8vo. 21s.
— Lalla Rookh, illustrated by Tenniel. Square crown 8vo. 10s. 6d.
New Testament (The) illustrated with Woodcuts after Paintings by the Early Masters. 4to. 21s. cloth, or 42s. morocco.
Perry on Greek and Roman Sculpture. With 280 Illustrations engraved on Wood. Square crown 8vo. 31s. 6d.

London, LONGMANS & CO.

THE USEFUL ARTS, MANUFACTURES, &c.

Bourne's Catechism of the Steam Engine. Fcp. 8vo. 6s.
— Examples of Steam, Air, and Gas Engines. 4to. 70s.
— Handbook of the Steam Engine. Fcp. 8vo. 9s.
— Recent Improvements in the Steam Engine. Fcp. 8vo. 6s.
— Treatise on the Steam Engine. 4to. 42s.
Cresy's Encyclopædia of Civil Engineering. 8vo. 25s.
Culley's Handbook of Practical Telegraphy. 8vo. 16s.
Eastlake's Household Taste in Furniture, &c. Square crown 8vo. 14s.
Fairbairn's Useful Information for Engineers. 3 vols. crown 8vo. 31s. 6d.
— Mills and Millwork. 1 vol. 8vo. 25s.
Gwilt's Encyclopædia of Architecture. 8vo. 52s. 6d.
Kerl's Metallurgy, adapted by Crookes and Röhrig. 3 vols. 8vo. £4. 19s.
Loudon's Encyclopædia of Agriculture. 8vo. 21s.
— — — Gardening. 8vo. 21s.
Mitchell's Manual of Practical Assaying. 8vo. 31s. 6d.
Northcott's Lathes and Turning. 8vo. 18s.
Payen's Industrial Chemistry Edited by B. H. Paul, Ph.D. 8vo. 42s.
Piesse's Art of Perfumery. Fourth Edition. Square crown 8vo. 21s.
Sennett's Treatise on the Marine Steam Engine. 8vo. 21s.
Ure's Dictionary of Arts, Manufactures, &. Mines. 4 vols. medium 8vo. £7. 7s.
Ville on Artificial Manures. By Crookes. 8vo. 21s.

RELIGIOUS AND MORAL WORKS.

Abbey & Overton's English Church in the Eighteenth Century. 2 vols. 8vo. 36s.
Arnold's (Rev. Dr. Thomas) Sermons. 6 vols. crown 8vo. 5s. each.
Bishop Jeremy Taylor's Entire Works. With Life by Bishop Heber. Edited by the Rev. C. P. Eden. 10 vols. 8vo. £5. 5s.
Boultbee's Commentary on the 39 Articles. Crown 8vo. 6s.
— History of the Church of England, Pre-Reformation Period. 8vo. 15s.
Bray's Elements of Morality. Fcp. 8vo. 2s. 6d.
Browne's (Bishop) Exposition of the 39 Articles. 8vo. 16s.
Calvert's Wife's Manual. Crown 8vo. 6s.
Christ our Ideal. 8vo. 8s. 6d.
Colenso's Lectures on the Pentateuch and the Moabite Stone. 8vo. 12s.
Colenso on the Pentateuch and Book of Joshua. Crown 8vo. 6s.
Conder's Handbook of the Bible. Post 8vo. 7s. 6d.
Conybeare & Howson's Life and Letters of St. Paul :—
   Library Edition, with all the Original Illustrations, Maps, Landscapes on Steel, Woodcuts, &c. 2 vols. 4to. 42s.
   Intermediate Edition, with a Selection of Maps, Plates, and Woodcuts. 2 vols. square crown 8vo. 21s.
   Student's Edition, revised and condensed, with 46 Illustrations and Maps. 1 vol. crown 8vo. 7s. 6d.
Creighton's History of the Papacy during the Reformation. 2 vols. 8vo. 32s.
Davidson's Introduction to the Study of the New Testament. 2 vols. 8vo. 30s.
Edersheim's Life and Times of Jesus the Messiah. 2 vols. 8vo. 42s.

London, LONGMANS & CO.

Ellicott's (Bishop) Commentary on St. Paul's Epistles. 8vo. Galatians, 8*s*. 6*d*. Ephesians, 8*s*. 6*d*. Pastoral Epistles, 10*s*. 6*d*. Philippians, Colossians and Philemon, 10*s*. 6*d*. Thessalonians, 7*s*. 6*d*.

Ellicott's Lectures on the Life of our Lord. 8vo. 12*s*.

Ewald's Antiquities of Israel, translated by Solly. 8vo. 12*s*. 6*d*.

— History of Israel, translated by Carpenter & Smith. 6 vols. 8vo. 79*s*.

Gospel (The) for the Nineteenth Century. 4th Edition. 8vo. 10*s*. 6*d*.

Hopkins's Christ the Consoler. Fcp. 8vo. 2*s*. 6*d*.

Jukes's New Man and the Eternal Life. Crown 8vo. 6*s*.

— Second Death and the Restitution of all Things. Crown 8vo. 3*s*. 6*d*.

— Types of Genesis. Crown 8vo. 7*s*. 6*d*.

Kalisch's Bible Studies. PART I. the Prophecies of Balaam. 8vo. 10*s*. 6*d*.

— — — PART II. the Book of Jonah. 8vo. 10*s*. 6*d*.

— Historical and Critical Commentary on the Old Testament; with a New Translation. Vol. I. *Genesis*, 8vo. 18*s*. or adapted for the General Reader, 12*s*. Vol. II. *Exodus*, 15*s*. or adapted for the General Reader, 12*s*. Vol. III. *Leviticus*, Part I. 15*s*. or adapted for the General Reader, 8*s*. Vol. IV. *Leviticus*, Part II. 15*s*. or adapted for the General Reader, 8*s*.

Keary's Outlines of Primitive Belief. 8vo. 18*s*.

Lyra Germanica : Hymns translated by Miss Winkworth. Fcp. 8vo. 5*s*.

Manning's Temporal Mission of the Holy Ghost. Crown 8vo. 8*s*. 6*d*.

Martineau's Endeavours after the Christian Life. Crown 8vo. 7*s*. 6*d*.

— Hymns of Praise and Prayer. Crown 8vo. 4*s*. 6*d*. 32mo. 1*s*. 6*d*.

— Sermons, Hours of Thought on Sacred Things. 2 vols. 7*s*. 6*d*. each.

Mill's Three Essays on Religion. 8vo. 10*s*. 6*d*.

Monsell's Spiritual Songs for Sundays and Holidays. Fcp. 8vo. 5*s*. 18mo. 2*s*.

Müller's (Max) Origin & Growth of Religion. Crown 8vo. 7*s*. 6*d*.

— — Science of Religion. Crown 8vo. 7*s*. 6*d*.

Newman's Apologia pro Vitâ Suâ. Crown 8vo. 6*s*.

Sewell's (Miss) Passing Thoughts on Religion. Fcp. 8vo. 3*s*. 6*d*.

— — Preparation for the Holy Communion. 32mo. 3*s*.

Seymour's Hebrew Psalter. Crown 8vo. 2*s*. 6*d*.

Smith's Voyage and Shipwreck of St. Paul. Crown 8vo. 7*s*. 6*d*.

Supernatural Religion. Complete Edition. 3 vols. 8vo. 36*s*.

Whately's Lessons on the Christian Evidences. 18mo. 6*d*.

White's Four Gospels in Greek, with Greek-English Lexicon. 32mo. 5*s*.

TRAVELS, VOYAGES, &c.

Aldridge's Ranch Notes in Kansas, Colorado, &c. Crown 8vo. 5*s*.

Baker's Eight Years in Ceylon. Crown 8vo. 5*s*.

— Rifle and Hound in Ceylon. Crown 8vo. 5*s*.

Ball's Alpine Guide. 3 vols. post 8vo. with Maps and Illustrations :—I. Western Alps, 6*s*. 6*d*. II. Central Alps, 7*s*. 6*d*. III. Eastern Alps, 10*s*. 6*d*.

Ball on Alpine Travelling, and on the Geology of the Alps, 1*s*.

Brassey's Sunshine and Storm in the East. Crown 8vo. 7*s*. 6*d*.

— Voyage in the Yacht 'Sunbeam.' Crown 8vo. 7*s*. 6*d*. School Edition, fcp. 8vo. 2*s*. Popular Edition, 4to. 6*d*.

Crawford's Across the Pampas and the Andes. Crown 8vo. 7*s*. 6*d*.

London, LONGMANS & CO.

Freeman's Impressions of the United States of America. Crown 8vo. 6s.
Hassall's San Remo Climatically considered. Crown 8vo. 5s.
Miller's Wintering in the Riviera. Post 8vo. Illustrations. 7s. 6d.
The Alpine Club Map of Switzerland. In Four Sheets. 42s.
Three in Norway. By Two of Them. Crown 8vo. Illustrations, 6s.

WORKS OF FICTION.

Brabourne's (Lord) Higgledy-Piggledy. Crown 8vo. 3s. 6d.
   —   —   Whispers from Fairy Land. Crown 8vo. 3s. 6d.
Cabinet Edition of Novels and Tales by the Earl of Beaconsfield, K.G. 11 vols.
     crown 8vo. price 6s. each.
Cabinet Edition of Stories and Tales by Miss Sewell. Crown 8vo. cloth extra,
     gilt edges, price 3s. 6d. each :—

Amy Herbert. Cleve Hall.	A Glimpse of the World.
The Earl's Daughter.	Katharine Ashton.
Experience of Life.	Laneton Parsonage.
Gertrude. Ivors.	Margaret Percival. Ursula.

Dissolving Views. A Novel. By Mrs. Andrew Lang. 2 vols. crown 8vo. 14s.
Novels and Tales by the Earl of Beaconsfield, K.G. Hughenden Edition, with 2
     Portraits on Steel and 11 Vignettes on Wood. 11 vols. crown 8vo. £2. 2s.
The Modern Novelist's Library. Each Work in crown 8vo. A Single Volume,
     complete in itself, price 2s. boards, or 2s. 6d. cloth :—

By the Earl of Beaconsfield, K.G.
     Lothair. Coningsby.
     Sybil. Tancred.
     Venetia. Henrietta Temple.
     Contarini Fleming.
     Alroy, Ixion, &c.
     The Young Duke, &c.
     Vivian Grey. Endymion.

By Bret Harte.
     In the Carquinez Woods.

By Mrs. Oliphant.
     In Trust, the Story of a Lady
     and her Lover.

By Anthony Trollope.
     Barchester Towers.
     The Warden.

By Major Whyte-Melville.
     Digby Grand.
     General Bounce.
     Kate Coventry.
     The Gladiators.
     Good for Nothing.
     Holmby House.
     The Interpreter.
     The Queen's Maries.

By Various Writers.
     The Atelier du Lys.
     Atherstone Priory.
     The Burgomaster's Family.
     Elsa and her Vulture.
     Mademoiselle Mori.
     The Six Sisters of the Valleys.
     Unawares.

In the Olden Time. By the Author of 'Mademoiselle Mori.' Crown 8vo. 6s.
Thicker than Water. By James Payn. Crown 8vo. 6s.

POETRY AND THE DRAMA.

Bailey's Festus, a Poem. Crown 8vo. 12s. 6d.
Bowdler's Family Shakspeare. Medium 8vo. 14s. 6 vols. fcp. 8vo. 21s.
Cayley's Iliad of Homer, Homometrically translated. 8vo. 12s. 6d.
Conington's Æneid of Virgil, translated into English Verse. Crown 8vo. 9s.
   —   Prose Translation of Virgil's Poems. Crown 8vo. 9s.
Goethe's Faust, translated by Birds. Large crown 8vo. 12s. 6d.
   —   —   translated by Webb. 8vo. 12s. 6d.
   —   —   edited by Selss. Crown 8vo. 5s.

London, LONGMANS & CO.

Homer's Iliad. Greek Text with Verse Translation by W. C. Green. Vol I. crown 8vo. 6s.

Ingelow's Poems. New Edition. 2 vols. fcp. 8vo. 12s.

Macaulay's Lays of Ancient Rome, with Ivry and the Armada. Illustrated by Weguelin. Crown 8vo. 3s. 6d. gilt edges.

The same, Annotated Edition, fcp. 8vo. 1s. sewed, 1s. 6d. cloth, 2s. 6d. cloth extra.

The same, Popular Edition. Illustrated by Scharf. Fcp. 4to. 6d. swd., 1s. cloth.

Pennell's (Cholmondeley-) 'From Grave to Gay.' A Volume of Selections. Fcp. 8vo. 6s.

Southey's Poetical Works. Medium 8vo. 14s.

RURAL SPORTS, HORSE AND CATTLE MANAGEMENT, &c.

Dead Shot (The), by Marksman. Crown 8vo. 10s. 6d.

Fitzwygram's Horses and Stables. 8vo. 10s. 6d.

Francis's Treatise on Fishing in all its Branches. Post 8vo. 15s.

Horses and Roads. By Free-Lance. Crown 8vo. 6s.

Howitt's Visits to Remarkable Places. Crown 8vo. 7s. 6d.

Jefferies' The Red Deer. Crown 8vo. 4s. 6d.

Miles's Horse's Foot, and How to Keep it Sound. Imperial 8vo. 12s. 6d.

— Plain Treatise on Horse-Shoeing. Post 8vo. 2s. 6d.

— Remarks on Horses' Teeth. Post 8vo. 1s. 6d.

— Stables and Stable-Fittings. Imperial 8vo. 15s.

Milner's Country Pleasures. Crown 8vo. 6s.

Nevile's Horses and Riding. Crown 8vo. 6s.

Ronalds's Fly-Fisher's Entomology. 8vo. 14s.

Steel's Diseases of the Ox, a Manual of Bovine Pathology. 8vo. 15s.

Stonehenge's Dog in Health and Disease. Square crown 8vo. 7s. 6d.

— Greyhound. Square crown 8vo. 15s.

Wilcocks's Sea-Fisherman. Post 8vo. 6s.

Youatt's Work on the Dog. 8vo. 6s.

— — — — Horse. 8vo. 7s. 6d.

WORKS OF UTILITY AND GENERAL INFORMATION.

Acton's Modern Cookery for Private Families. Fcp. 8vo. 4s. 6d.

Black's Practical Treatise on Brewing. 8vo. 10s. 6d.

Buckton's Food and Home Cookery. Crown 8vo. 2s. 6d.

Bull on the Maternal Management of Children. Fcp. 8vo. 1s. 6d.

Bull's Hints to Mothers on the Management of their Health during the Period of Pregnancy and in the Lying-in Room. Fcp. 8vo. 1s. 6d.

Burton's My Home Farm. Crown 8vo. 3s. 6d.

Campbell-Walker's Correct Card, or How to Play at Whist. Fcp. 8vo. 2s. 6d.

Edwards' Our Seamarks. Crown 8vo. 8s. 6d.

Johnson's (W. & J. H.) Patentee's Manual. Fourth Edition. 8vo. 10s. 6d.

— — The Patents Designs &c. Act, 1883. Fcp. 8vo. 1s.

Longman's Chess Openings. Fcp. 8vo. 2s. 6d.

Macleod's Elements of Banking. Fourth Edition. Crown 8vo. 5s.

— Elements of Economics. 2 vols. small crown 8vo. VOL. I. 7s. 6d.

— Theory and Practice of Banking. 2 vols. 8vo. Vol. I. 12s.

London, LONGMANS & CO.

M'Culloch's Dictionary of Commerce and Commercial Navigation. 8vo. 63*.
Maunder's Biographical Treasury. Fcp. 8vo. 6*.
—   Historical Treasury. Fcp. 8vo. 6*.
—   Scientific and Literary Treasury. Fcp. 8vo. 6*.
—   Treasury of Bible Knowledge, edited by Ayre. Fcp. 8vo. 6*.
—   Treasury of Botany, edited by Lindley & Moore. Two Parts, 12*.
—   Treasury of Geography. Fcp. 8vo. 6*.
—   Treasury of Knowledge and Library of Reference. Fcp. 8vo. 6*.
—   Treasury of Natural History. Fcp. 8vo. 6*.
Pole's Theory of the Modern Scientific Game of Whist. Fcp. 8vo. 2*. 6d.
Quain's Dictionary of Medicine. Medium 8vo. 31*. 6d. or in 2 vols. 34*.
Reeve's Cookery and Housekeeping. Crown 8vo. 7*. 6d.
Scott's Farm Valuer. Crown 8vo. 5*.
Smith's Handbook for Midwives. Crown 8vo. 5*.
The Cabinet Lawyer, a Popular Digest of the Laws of England. Fcp. 8vo. 9*.
Ville on Artificial Manures, by Crookes. 8vo. 21*.
Willich's Popular Tables, by Marriott. Crown 8vo. 10*.

MUSICAL WORKS BY JOHN HULLAH, LL.D.

Hullah's Method of Teaching Singing. Crown 8vo. 2*. 6d.
Exercises and Figures in the same. Crown 8vo. 1*. sewed, or 1*. 2d. limp cloth ; or 2 Parts, 6d. each sewed, or 8d. each limp cloth.
Large Sheets, containing the 'Exercises and Figures in Hullah's Method,' in Five Parcels of Eight Sheets each, price 6*. each.
Chromatic Scale, with the Inflected Syllables, on Large Sheet. 1*. 6d.
Card of Chromatic Scale. 1d.
Grammar of Musical Harmony. Royal 8vo. price 3*. sewed and 4*. 6d. cloth ; or in 2 Parts, each 1*. 6d.
Exercises to Grammar of Musical Harmony. 1*.
Grammar of Counterpoint. Part I. super-royal 8vo. 2*. 6d.
Wilhem's Manual of Singing. Parts I. & II. 2*. 6d. each or together, 5*.
Exercises and Figures contained in Parts I. and II. of Wilhem's Manual. Books I. & II. each 8d.
Large Sheets, Nos. 1 to 8, containing the Figures in Part I. of Wilhem's Manual, in a Parcel, 6*.
Large Sheets, Nos. 9 to 40, containing the Exercises in Part I. of Wilhem's Manual, in Four Parcels of Eight Nos. each, per Parcel, 6*.
Large Sheets, Nos. 41 to 52, containing the Figures in Part II. In a Parcel, 9*.
Hymns for the Young, set to Music. Royal 8vo. 8d. sewed, or 1*. 6d. cloth.
Infant School Songs. 6d.
Notation, the Musical Alphabet. Crown 8vo. 6d.
Old English Songs for Schools, Harmonised. 6d.
Rudiments of Musical Grammar. Royal 8vo. 3*.
School Songs for 2 and 3 Voices. 2 Books, 8vo. each 6d.
Lectures on the History of Modern Music. 8vo. 8*. 6d.
Lectures on the Transition Period of Musical History. 8vo. 10*. 6d.

London, LONGMANS & CO.

Spottiswoode & Co. Printers, New-street Square, London.